Misguided Angel

a Blue Bloods novel

MELISSA DE LA CRUZ

HYPERION
New York

First Edition
1 3 5 7 9 10 8 6 4 2
V567-9638-5-10227
Printed in the United States of America
This book is set in 12-point Baskerville.
Designed by Elizabeth H. Clark

Library of Congress Cataloging-in-Publication Data on file.
ISBN 978-1-4231-2128-2
Reinforced binding

Visit www.hyperionteens.com

THIS LABEL APPLIES TO TEXT STOCK

For Pop,
Alberto B. de la Cruz,
September 7, 1949–October 25, 2009,
who thought Dedications and Acknowledgments
were the best part of my books because he was always in them

Misguided angel hanging over me,
Heart like a Gabriel, pure and white as ivory
Soul like a Lucifer, black and cold like a piece of lead.
Misguided angel, love you till I'm dead.

—Cowboy Junkies, "Misguided Angel"

All things change, nothing perishes.

—Ovid

November 11, 2005

There were seven of us at the inception of the order. A conclave was called to address the growing threat posed by the Paths of the Dead. Along with myself, present at the gathering were the Emperor's cousin Gemellus, a weakling; Octilla and Halcyon from the vestal virgins; General Alexandrus, head of the Imperial Army; Pantaelum, a trusted senator; and Onbasius, a healer.

In my prodigious research I have determined that Halcyon was most likely the keeper of the Gate of Promise, the third known Gate of Hell. I have come to the conclusion that this gate is instrumental in uncovering the truth behind the continued existence of our supposedly vanquished enemies. This is the gate we must focus on, the most important one in the lot.

From what I can deduce, Halcyon settled in Florence, and it is my belief that her latest recorded incarnation was as Catherine of Siena, a famous Italian mystic "born" in 1347. However, after Catherine's "death," there is no other record of a prominent female presence in the city. It appears she had no heirs to her name, and her line simply disappears after the end of Giovanni de Medici's rule in 1429.

From the fifteenth century onward, the city becomes the center of the growing power of the Petruvian Order, founded by the ambitious priest Father Benedictus Linardi. The Petruvian school and monastery are currently under the leadership of one Father Roberto Baldessarre. I have written to Father Baldessarre and leave for Florence tomorrow.

A Chase

The sound of footsteps on cobblestone echoed throughout the empty streets of the city. Tomasia kept the pace, her kidskin slippers hardly making a sound, while behind her came the slap of Andreas's heavy boots and Giovanni's lighter step. They ran in a single file, a tight unit, used to this kind of discipline, used to blending in with the dark. When they arrived at the middle of the square, they separated.

Tomi flew up the nearest cornerstone and perched on a cornice looking over the broad panorama of the city: the half-built dome of the Basilica to the Ponte Vecchio and beyond the river. She sensed the creature was near and prepared to strike. Their target still did not know he was being followed, and her blow would be immediate and invisible, every trace of the Silver Blood eradicated and extinguished—almost as if the beast—disguised as a palace guard—never existed. Even the creature's last gasp must be silent. Tomasia kept her position, waiting for the creature to come to her, to walk into the trap they had laid.

She heard Dre grunting, a bit out of breath, and then next to him,

Gio, his sword already unsheathed, as they followed the vampire into the alley.

This was her chance. She flew down from her hiding place, holding her dagger with her teeth.

But when she landed, the creature was nowhere to be found.

"Where——?" she asked, but Gio put a finger to his mouth and motioned to the alleyway.

Tomi raised her eyebrows. This was unusual. The Silver Blood had stopped to converse with a hooded stranger. Strange: the Croatan despised the Red Bloods and avoided them unless they were torturing them for sport.

"Should we?" she asked, moving toward the alley.

"Wait," Andreas ordered. He was nineteen, tall and broad, with sculpted muscles and a ferocious brow—handsome and ruthless. He was their leader, and had always been.

Next to him, Gio looked elfin, almost fey, with a beauty that could not be denied or hidden under his scraggly beard and long, unkempt hair. He kept his hand on his weapon, tense and ready to spring.

Tomi did the same, and caressed the sharp edge of her dagger. It made her feel better to know it was there.

"Let's watch what happens," Dre decided.

PART THE FIRST

SCHUYLER VAN ALEN AND THE GATE OF PROMISE

Off the Italian Coast

The Present

ONE

The Cinque Terre

*S*chuyler Van Alen walked as quickly as she could up the polished brass spiral stairs leading to the upper deck. Jack Force was standing at the edge of the bow when she caught his eye. She nodded to him, shielding her eyes from the hot Mediterranean sun. *It's done.*

Good, he sent, and went back to setting the anchor. He was sunburned and shaggy, his skin a deep nut brown, his hair the color of flax. Her own dark hair was wild and unkempt from a month of salty sea air. She wore an old shirt of Jack's that had once been white and pristine and was now gray and ragged at the hems. They both displayed that laconic, relaxed air affected by those on perpetual vacation: a lazy, weathered aimlessness that belied their true desperation. A month was long enough. They had to act now. They had to act today.

The muscles on Jack's arms tensed as he tugged on the

rope to see if the anchor had found purchase on the ocean floor. No luck. The anchor heaved, so he released the line a few more feet. He raised a finger over his right shoulder, signaling to Schuyler to reverse the port engine. He let the rope go a little farther and tugged at it again, the stout white braids of the anchor line chafing his palm as he pulled it toward him.

From her summers sailing on Nantucket, Schuyler knew that an ordinary man would have used a motor winch to set the seven-hundred-pound anchor, but of course Jack was far from ordinary. He pulled harder—using almost all of his strength, and all eight tons of the Countess's yacht seemed to flex for a moment. This time the anchor held, wedged into the rocky bottom. Jack relaxed and dropped the rope, and Schuyler moved from the helm to help him twine it around the base of the winch. In the past month they'd each found quiet solace in these small tasks. It gave them something to do while they plotted their escape.

For while Isabelle of Orleans had welcomed them to the safety of her home, Jack remembered that once upon a time, in another lifetime, Isabelle had been Lucifer's beloved, Drusilla, sister-wife to the emperor Caligula. True, the Countess had been more than generous toward them: she had blessed them with every comfort—the boat, in particular, was fully staffed and bountifully stocked. Yet it was becoming clearer each day that the Countess's offer of protection was morphing from asylum to confinement. It was already November and they were virtual prisoners in her care, as they were never left alone, nor were they allowed to leave. Schuyler and Jack were as far from finding the Gate of Promise as they had been when they'd left New York.

The Countess had given them everything except what they needed most: freedom. Schuyler did not believe that Isabelle, who had been a great friend to Lawrence and Cordelia, and was one of the most respected vampire dowagers of European society, was a Silver Blood traitor. But of course, given the recent events, anything seemed possible. In any event, if the Countess was planning on keeping them prisoner for perpetuity, they couldn't afford to wait and find out.

Schuyler glanced shyly at Jack. They had been together a month now, but even though they were finally an official couple, everything felt so new—his touch, his voice, his companionship, the easy feel of his arm around her shoulder. She stood beside him against the rail, and he looped his arm around her neck, pulling her closer so he could plant a quick kiss on the top of her head. She liked those kisses the most, found a deep contentment at the confident way he held her. They belonged to each other now.

Maybe this was what Allegra had meant, Schuyler thought, when she had told her to come home and stop fighting, stop fleeing from finding her own happiness. Maybe this was what her mother wanted her to understand.

Jack lowered his arm from her shoulder, and she followed

his gaze to the small rowboat "the boys" were lowering from the stern onto the choppy water below. They were a jolly duo, two Italians, Drago and Iggy (short for Ignazio), Venators in service to the Countess and, for all intents and purposes, Jack and Schuyler's jailers. But Schuyler had come to like them almost as friends, and the thought of what she and Jack were about to do set her nerves on edge. She hoped the Venators would be spared from harm, but she and Jack would do what they had to. She marveled at his calm demeanor; she herself could barely keep still, bouncing up and down on the balls of her feet in anticipation.

She followed Jack to the edge of the platform. Iggy had tethered the little boat to the yacht, and Drago reached forward to help Schuyler step down. But Jack slipped ahead and brushed Drago aside so he could offer Schuyler his palm instead, ever the gentleman. She held his hand as she climbed over the rail and into the boat. Drago shrugged and steadied the boat as Iggy brought the last of the provisions onto the bow—several picnic baskets and backpacks filled with blankets and water. Schuyler patted her bag, confirming that the Repository files with Lawrence's notes were in their usual place.

Schuyler turned to look closely upon the rugged Italian coast for the first time. Ever since they had learned of Iggy's affinity for the Cinque Terre, they had been advocating for this little day trip. The Cinque Terre was a strip of the Italian Riviera populated by a series of five medieval towns.

Iggy, with his broad face and fat belly, spoke longingly of running along the paths along the cliff edge before coming home to outdoor dinners overlooking sunsets above the bay.

She had never been to this part of Italy and did not know too much about it—but she understood how they could use Iggy's affection for his hometown to their advantage. He had not been able to resist their suggestion to visit, and allowed them a day off of their floating prison. It was the perfect spot for what they had planned, as trails ended in ancient stairs that stretched upward for hundreds of feet. The paths would be abandoned this time of year—tourist season was over, as fall brought cold weather to the popular resort towns. The mountain trails would lead them far from the ship.

"You are going to love this place, Jack," Iggy said, rowing vigorously. "You too, *signorina*," he said. The Italians had a difficult time pronouncing *Schuyler*.

Jack grunted, pulling on his oar, and Schuyler tried to affect a festive air. They were supposed to be getting ready for a picnic. Schuyler noticed Jack brooding, staring at the sea, preparing himself for the day ahead, and she swatted his arm playfully. This was supposed to be a long-awaited respite from their time on the ship, a chance to spend a day exploring.

They were supposed to look like a happy couple with not a care in the world, not like two captives about to execute a prison break.

*S*chuyler felt her mood lift as they pulled into the bay at Vernazza. The view could bring a smile to anyone's face, and even Jack brightened. The rock ledges were spectacular and the houses that clung to them looked as ancient as the stones themselves. They docked the boat, and the foursome hiked up the cliff side toward the trail.

The five towns that formed the Cinque Terre were connected by a series of stony paths, some almost impossible to climb, Iggy explained, as they walked past a succession of tiny stucco homes. The Venator was in a jubilant mood, telling them the history of every house they walked past. "And this one, my aunty Clara sold in 1977 to a nice family from Parma, and this right here was where the most beautiful girl in Italy lived"—Iggy made a kissing noise—"but . . . Red Blood lady you know how they are . . . *picky* . . . Oh and this is where . . ."

Iggy called out to farmers as they walked through the backyards and fields, patting animals as they strolled past their pastures. The trail wound back and forth from grassland to homes to the very edge of the sea cliffs.

Schuyler watched tiny rocks tumble over the side of the hill as they made their way forward. Iggy kept the conversation flowing, while Drago nodded and laughed to himself, as if he had taken the tour one time too many and was merely humoring his friend. The climb was hard work, but Schuyler was glad for the chance to stretch her muscles, and she was certain Jack was too. They had spent too much time on the boat, and while they had been allowed to swim in the ocean, it wasn't the same as a good hike in the open air. In a few hours they had moved from Vernazza to Corniglia and then Manarola. Schuyler noticed that they passed the day without seeing a single car or truck, not a phone line or power cable.

This is it, Jack sent. *Over there.*

Schuyler knew it meant he had judged their distance to be nearly halfway between the last two towns. It was time. Schuyler tapped Iggy on the shoulder and gestured toward a craggy outcropping that hung over the cliff side. "Lunch?" she asked, her eyes twinkling.

Iggy smiled. "Of course! In all my exuberance I forgot to let us stop and eat!"

The spot Schuyler had led them to was in a peculiar location. The trail stretched out toward a promontory so that there were cliffs on either side of the narrow path.

The two Venators spread one of the Countess's spotless white tablecloths over a grassy plateau between the rough stone, and the four of them crammed into the small space. Schuyler tried not to look down as she snuggled up as close to the edge as possible.

Jack sat across from her, gazing over her shoulder at the shoreline below. He kept his eyes on the beach as Schuyler helped unpack the basket. She brought out salamis and prosciutto di Parma, finocchiona, mortadella, and air-cured beef. Some of the meat came in long rolls, while others were cut into small disks and wrapped in wax paper. There was a loaf of rosemary cake, along with a brown paper bag full of almond tarts and jam crostata. It was a pity it was all going to go to waste. Drago pulled several plastic containers filled with Italian cheeses—pecorino and fresh burrata wrapped in green asphodel leaves. Schuyler tore off a piece of the burrata and took a bite. It was buttery and milky, equal to the view in splendor.

She caught Jack's eyes briefly. *Get ready*, he sent. She continued to smile and eat, even as her stomach clenched. She turned briefly to see what Jack had seen. A small motorboat had pulled up to the beach below. Who would have known a teenage North African pirate from the Somali coast would prove to be such a reliable contact, Schuyler thought. Even from far above she could see that he had brought them what they had asked for: one of the pirate crew's fastest speedboats, jerry-rigged with a grossly oversized engine.

Iggy popped open a bottle of Prosecco, and the four of them toasted the sun-drenched coastline with friendly smiles. He lifted his hand in a wide gesture as he gazed down at the midday feast. "Shall we begin?"

That was the moment she had been waiting for. Schuyler sprang into action. She leaned back and appeared to lose her balance for a moment, then bent forward and tossed the full contents of her wineglass into Drago's face. The alcohol stung his eyes, and he looked baffled, but before he could react, Iggy slapped him on the back and guffawed heartily, as if Schuyler had made a particularly funny joke.

With Drago momentarily blinded, and Iggy's eyes closed in laughter, Jack moved to strike. He slid a shank out from his shirtsleeve and into his palm, flipped it around and drove the knife deep into Drago's chest, sending the Italian sprawling to the ground, bleeding. Schuyler had helped Jack make the blade from one of the deck boards. He had hollowed out the back of a loose stair tread and carved it against a stone she'd found on a dive. The shank was made from ironwood, and it made for a dangerous and deadly little dagger.

Schuyler rushed for the other Venator, but Iggy was gone before she could stand. This they had not counted on. The fat man could *move*. In an instant he had pulled the shank from his friend's chest to use as a weapon of his own and turned toward Schuyler, the laughter having died from his eyes.

"Jack!" she cried as the Venator charged. She suddenly couldn't move. Iggy had hit her with a stasis spell when he'd stolen the blade, which he was now holding above her chest. In a moment it would pierce her heart—but Jack dove between them and took the full brunt of the blow.

Schuyler had to get out of the spell. She wrenched herself forward with every ounce of energy, fighting the invisible web that held her. The sensation was like moving in slow motion through a thick ooze, but she found the spell's weak link and broke through. She screamed as she ran toward Jack's seemingly lifeless body.

Iggy got there first, but as he turned Jack over, he did a double take. Jack was unharmed, alive, and smiling grimly.

He leapt to his feet. "Tsk, tsk, Venator. How could you forget an angel cannot be harmed with a blade of his own making?" Jack rolled up his sleeves as he faced his adversary. "Why don't you make it easy on yourself?" he said mildly. "I suggest you go back and tell the Countess that we are not a pair of trinkets she can keep in a jewelry box. Go now, and we will leave you unharmed."

For a moment it appeared as if the Venator was about to consider the offer, but Schuyler knew he was too old a soul to take such a cowardly route. The Italian removed a nasty-looking curved blade from his pocket and pounced toward Jack, but suddenly stopped in midair. He hung there for second with a funny look on his face, part confusion and part defeat.

"Nice move with the stasis," Jack said, turning to Schuyler.

"Anytime." She smiled. She had taken the edges of the

spell that had paralyzed her and hit the Venator with it.

Jack took it from there, and with a powerful gesture, he threw the fat guard off the side of the cliff, sending him crashing to the water below. Schuyler rolled the unconscious Drago to the edge and threw him over as well, to join his friend in the ocean.

"You got the tank?" Jack asked as they scrambled down the face of the cliff to the pirate boat waiting for them below.

"Of course." She nodded. They had planned their escape well: Jack had driven the yacht's anchor impossibly deep into the rocky ocean bottom, while Schuyler had emptied the yacht's fuel supply. The night before they had sabotaged the boat's sails and the radio.

They ran across the beach toward the pirate boat, where their new friend Ghedi was waiting for them. Schuyler had befriended him during one of their supervised trips to the Saint-Tropez market, where the former member of the self-styled "Somali Marines" was helping unload a pallet of fresh fish upon the dock. Ghedi missed his days of adventure and jumped at the chance to help the two trapped Americans.

"All yours, bossing." Ghedi smiled, showing a row of gleaming white teeth. He was lithe and quick, with a merry, handsome face and skin the color of burnished cocoa. He jumped off the starboard. He would catch a ride back to the market on the ferry.

"Thanks, man," Jack said, taking the wheel. "Check your accounts tomorrow."

The Somali grinned more widely, and Schuyler knew the fun of stealing the boat was almost payment enough.

The massive engine roared to life as they sped away from the shore. Schuyler glanced to where the two Venators were floating lifelessly in the water. She comforted herself with the knowledge that both would survive. They were ancient creatures and no cliff-side fall could truly harm them; only their egos would be bruised. Still, they wouldn't be able to recover for a while, and by then she and Jack would be well on their way.

She exhaled. Finally. On to Florence, to begin the search for the keepers and secure the gate before the Silver Bloods found it. They were back on track.

"All right?" Jack asked, guiding the ship with expert ease through the stormy waves. He reached for her hand and squeezed it tightly.

She held it against her cheek, loving the feel of his rough calluses against her skin. They had done it. They were together. Safe. Free. Then she froze. "Jack, behind us."

"I know. I hear the engines," he said, without even bothering to look over his shoulder.

Schuyler stared at the horizon, where three dark shapes had appeared. More Venators, on Jet Skis with a black-and-silver cross insignia emblazoned on the windshields. Their forms grew larger and larger as they drew closer. Apparently Iggy and Drago hadn't been their only jailers.

Escape was going to be harder than they thought.

THREE

Into the Deep

The first drops of rain fell like gentle kisses on her cheek, and Schuyler hoped it would be nothing but a mild shower. But a glance at the ever-darkening sky told her otherwise. The calm blue horizon was now a palette of gray, red, and black; the clouds swirled together to form a heavy, solid mass. The rain, which had begun like a quiet afterthought, suddenly drummed against the deck in a rising staccato. The thunder cracked, a deep rumbling boom that made her jump.

Of course it had to rain. Just to make everything more complicated. Schuyler reached behind Jack and holstered a short bow they had asked Ghedi to procure and stow in the smuggler's locker, a hidden compartment located in the bilge.

During their month at sea they had passed the time by preparing for this escape. After hours, Jack had schooled

19

Schuyler in the fine points of Venator craft (subterfuge, ammunition), and with Iggy's and Drago's approval, had taught Schuyler a rudimentary course in archery. With her steady hand and eye, she had proven an even better shot than Jack. She removed several ironwood arrows from her pack, more handmade weapons fashioned during their captivity. Schuyler holstered one against the bow and took position.

Their pursuers were still a long way behind for now. She could see them clearly even through the wind and fog. She bent her knees slightly and willed herself to be a statue in the moving sea, raising the bow and drawing the arrow as far back as she could. When she was sure she had her mark, she let it fly. But the Jet Ski expertly dodged away.

Unperturbed, she reloaded the bow. This time when she drew the arrow, it lodged in a Venator's knee. The Jet Ski swerved uncontrollably in the water, and Schuyler felt triumphant until the Venator righted again, unfazed by his gaping wound.

Meanwhile, Jack kept his eyes straight ahead, a steady hand on the throttle. He was giving the engine everything it had, and it was burning up too fast and too hot—throwing off a shower of sparks and making a horrid sputtering noise.

Schuyler looked behind them again. Their pirate boat was doing the best it could, but it wouldn't be long before they were overtaken. The Venators were much closer now, no more than fifty feet away. It rained even harder, and she and Jack were both soaked to the bone as the wind whipped

20

up the waves and the boat rose and fell in a treacherous, roller-coaster fashion.

She planted her feet, hoping to get more leverage, as columns of water surged onto the deck. She only had two arrows left; she had to make them count. She armed up and poised to strike, just in time to see something fiery and blazing aimed right at her.

"Schuyler!" Jack yelled, pulling her down just as something exploded in the air where she had been standing. Good God, the Venators were fast—she hadn't even seen her assailant take aim and fire.

Jack kept one hand on the steering wheel, the other hand he kept protectively at her back. "Hellfire," he muttered as another explosion barely missed the starboard and shook the ship. The missiles were outfitted with the deadliest weapon in the Venators' arsenal: the Black Fire of Hell, the only thing on earth that could end the immortal blood running in their veins.

"But why would they want us dead?" Schuyler asked, above the roar of the storm as she held the bow to her side. Surely the Countess did not wish them that much ill will. Did she hate them that much?

"We're collateral damage now," Jack said. "She was only keeping us alive while it was convenient for her. But now that we've escaped, her ego can't take it. She'll kill us just to make a point. That no one defies the Countess."

The boat bounced across the swelling waves, each time

landing with a hard jolt, a rickety crunch of bolt and nail against wood and water. The engine was shot. It felt as if it was only by their sheer will that the makeshift speedboat held together.

Another blast rocked the helm of the ship, closer this time. The next one would sink them. Schuyler leapt from her hiding place, and in quick inhuman succession, pulled off the last two shafts. This time her arrows pierced the gas tank of the nearest Jet Ski, which exploded upon impact.

They didn't have time to celebrate, as another missile sailed over the bow, and Jack turned the wheel sharply to the right only to come directly upon a ten-foot-tall wave that swallowed the ship whole.

The pirate boat burst through to the other side, miraculously still intact.

Schuyler looked over her shoulder. Two Venators left; they were so close she could see the outline of their goggles and the silver stitching on their leather gloves. The Venators' faces were impassive. They didn't care if she and Jack lived or died, if they were innocent or guilty. They only took orders, and their orders were to shoot to kill.

A crashing wave took them precariously off balance, the ship tilting forward until it was almost vertical, then slammed back hard on the opposite end. Any moment now they were bound to capsize. They were out of arrows. They were out of options.

We'll have to ditch the ship. We'll go faster if we swim, Schuyler sent. It was the same thing Jack was thinking, she knew. It was just hard for him to say it. Because swimming meant being separated from each other. *Don't worry. I am strong. As are you.* She exchanged a wry smile with her love.

Jack gripped the steering wheel, his jaw clenched. *You're sure?*

Meet me in Genoa, she told him. The nearest coastal town from their current location. Thirty miles to the north.

He nodded, and a picture appeared in her mind, to show he knew it as well. A crowded port city ringed by mountains, colorful boats of every stripe bobbing in the harbor. From there they could hike through the rugged terrain to Florence.

Swim out as far as you can. I'll aim the ship at the remaining Jet Skis, Jack sent. He held her gaze for a moment.

Schuyler nodded.

On my count.

I can do this, Schuyler thought. I know I will see Jack again. I believe it.

There wasn't any time for a last kiss, or a last word of any sort. She felt Jack's countdown more than heard it— her body executing the commands before her brain could register them. By "three" she was already diving off the edge, already plowing down into the deep, dark water, already kicking her legs against the tide, already measuring her breath. As a vampire she could swim underwater for longer stretches than her human counterparts—but she would have to be careful not to waste energy.

Above the surface she heard a sickening crash as the pirate ship slammed into their enemies. The darkness of the sea was absolute, but after a while Schuyler's eyes adjusted. She pushed her hands against the water, churning, churning, muscles pushing and aching against the heavy water. She watched the bubbles rise to the surface. She could go five minutes without air, and she had to make good use of it. At last her lungs screamed for oxygen, and she began to kick up toward the surface—she had no desire now except to breathe—so close—so close—yes—one more kick and she would break through—yes. . . .

A cold, bony hand grasped her ankle, keeping her down, pulling her back into the deep.

Schuyler squirmed and kicked. She twisted so that she could see who was holding her. Below, a female Venator seemed to float effortlessly in the dark water. Her attacker assessed her coolly and continued to pull. *You are under the protection of the Countess. To deny this protection is an act against the Coven. Submit or be destroyed.*

The hand gripped her ankle in a solid lock. Schuyler could feel herself weakening—she would pass out soon if she didn't get air. Her lungs were about to burst. She was dizzy and starting to panic. Stop it, she told herself. She had to be calm.

The glom. Use the glom. *RELEASE ME*, she demanded, sending a compulsion so strong she could feel the words taking physical form, each letter an attack upon the Venator's cerebellum. The hand on her ankle shook slightly, and that was all Schuyler needed.

She burst away just as the Venator sent a compulsion of her own. Schuyler ducked and sent it back tenfold.

SINK!

The compulsion was a punch to the stomach, and the Venator flew backward into the deep, as if propelled downward by a sinking cannonball tied to her ankle. It would take her to the very bottom of the ocean, hopefully giving Schuyler enough time to get away.

She scrambled to get above the waves, finally breaking through to the surface, gasping for air. The rain, cold as a dead man's fingers, lashed her cheeks. She chanced a look back.

Their little motorboat was on fire. Burning, with sparks of black flames shooting up toward the heavens.

Jack made it out, she told herself. Of course he did. He had to.

A few feet away, Schuyler could see another Jet Ski circling the fiery carcass. But why hadn't that Venator gone after Jack, Schuyler wondered. Unless . . . unless he was already . . .

She couldn't finish the thought.

She wouldn't.

She pushed her head underneath the waves. The Genoa port. She began to swim.

FOUR

Driftwood

*E*verything around Schuyler was black, as dark above as below. If she swam below the ocean's surface she found she could make better time, and took to swimming deep underwater for longer and longer periods. Schuyler pushed against the current, buffeted by the waves; she felt as insignificant as flotsam, just another piece of ocean rubbish lost in the tide. She had to fight the desire to give in, to stop swimming, to close her eyes and rest and drown.

The storm broke for a moment, and Schuyler, bobbing up, could see the city rising from the water, its cheerful pastel buildings only a few hundred feet away. The midday sun was shining brightly on the pretty waterfront cafés. It was past high season, and the weather was brisk, so the outdoor tables were empty.

Schuyler tread water furiously to keep her head above the waves. God, she was tired. She was so close, but she didn't know if she could make it.

That was the problem with the *Velox*, Lawrence had warned her. You begin to believe in your superhuman capabilities, but the *Velox* demands rest, and it will have it whether you liked it or not. He had warned her of vampires who had pushed themselves to the limit, only to collapse at a crucial juncture and be overtaken by the Silver Bloods.

She had no more energy left; she couldn't propel herself the last few tantalizing feet to reach her goal.

She felt as limp as plankton. All the strength had drained from her body. She had covered about twenty-five miles in half an hour, but it wasn't enough to get her onto that nearby beach. She spit out some salt water and pushed her bangs out of her eyes, dog-paddling listlessly. Her muscles were torn, spent. She couldn't do one more stroke. . . .

An idea came to her. . . . She couldn't push forward anymore, but she could float. . . . She could just lie down, really, and let the waves do the rest. The thought of back-stroking the rest of the way struck her as incredibly ironic after the intensity of her escape. Well, she could float or she could drown. Just as she'd hoped, the slow steady movement required only the amount of energy that she could provide.

A few minutes after setting off at a leisurely pace, she felt the water around her vibrate, and she heard the distinctive motor of a Jet Ski. For a moment she was seized with fear; she kicked upright, looking all around, and then she saw it. Approaching quickly was a familiar vehicle branded with the dreaded black-and-silver cross, but that was no Venator at the helm.

Schuyler bounced up and down on the waves. "GHEDI! GHEDI!" She had no idea how the pirate had come to be on the Jet Ski, but right then she didn't care. All she knew was she had to get his attention before he got too far away.

He couldn't hear her, and the Jet Ski was getting farther and farther away.

GHEDI. TURN BACK. I COMMAND YOU.

The Jet Ski swung around, and in a moment, had roared up next to her. "*Signorina!* There you are!" he said, his bright smile splitting his face.

She pulled herself up next to him, thankful to be out of the water at last. "What are you doing here? Where's Jack?"

Ghedi shook his head. After he had bid them good-bye at the Cinque Terre, he had seen the Venators chase after them. He'd tried to radio them a warning, but the storm had taken out the satellite signals. He'd borrowed a motorboat, and had come upon the wreckage of the pirate ship ("Black, black smoke. Bad.") There had been no sign of Jack, and he'd taken an empty Jet Ski that was most likely left behind by the Venator who had chased Schuyler and who was probably still struggling to swim to the surface.

If Ghedi was here with this Jet Ski, then where was the other Jet Ski with the other Venator, Schuyler wondered. And where was Jack?

* * *

They circled the shoreline for several hours. It would be evening soon. Jack should be here by now, Schuyler thought. It would take a vampire of his speed only minutes to make it. She had managed, and he was by far a stronger swimmer. Schuyler dropped Ghedi off at the harbor, and she continued on the Jet Ski alone, as her new friend was showing signs of fatigue from their search. It wasn't fair to ask him to accompany her on what was looking more and more like a hopeless endeavor.

The sun slipped below the horizon, and the lights of the city looked festive against the purple sky. Music wafted from the restaurants and cafés by the docks. It was getting colder, and the wind told her the storm would pick up again soon; this was just a momentary calm.

She was going to run out of gas soon, but she made one last round. The night before, she and Jack had made a promise to each other. Whatever happened today, they had agreed they would not wait for the other if they were separated. The journey must continue, regardless of who kept on the path. Whoever remained would carry on Lawrence's legacy.

Okay, Jack, she thought. This is it. You'd better show up or I'm leaving.

She didn't want to think of what it meant, leaving him. She was terrified of being alone, now that she knew what being with Jack was like. He would want her to continue, though. He would want her to leave him, to go ahead without him. She had already wasted enough time.

She would ask Ghedi to help her get to Florence, where Lawrence believed the Gate of Promise was located; she would hike through the mountains as they'd planned. There would be no trains, no little *pensiones*, no rental cars, nothing that would leave a trail. Jack would be able to meet up with her later . . . maybe. . . .

Schuyler tried not to think about it too much. She felt numb from the cold and from what she would have to do. The enormity of her task felt overwhelming. How could she go on alone without knowing what had happened to him, without knowing if he was dead or alive?

Finally she saw it—it looked like driftwood but something about it caught her eye. Anxiously, she came up on it and saw that it was indeed just a piece of driftwood. But clinging to the center of it was a white hand, while the rest of the body was submerged underwater. Schuyler pulled up next to it; she recognized those long, thin fingers, and her heart beat against her chest, the cold creeping through her entire body. Fear. Abject fear.

Jack can't die. He can't die, but he can be harmed. He was immortal, but if it was too late to revive his physical shell, she would have to keep his blood for the next cycle. By the time he was reborn she would be at the end of hers. Who knew if he would love her then? If he would even remember her? In any event, where would she even take his blood? They were fugitives from the vampire community.

She leaned down and grasped his hand, pulling it gently from the branch. The hand was practically frozen in place, but it returned her grasp and squeezed. He was alive. With all her strength she pulled Jack out of the water in one quick motion and positioned him behind her on the Jet Ski.

He fell against her, his body as cold as an iceberg, and she could feel the weight of his exhaustion against her back. He was barely able to keep his arms around her waist as she pushed off into the darkness.

If she had been just a minute later, who knows what would have become of him. . . . Who knew what would have happened. . . . Who knew what . . .

Stop your doubting, my love. I knew you would find me.

Schuyler maneuvered the Jet Ski between two fishing boats and harnessed her craft next to the one that smelled marginally better than the other. The boats were empty, as fishing season was over. The owners would not return until next year. She helped Jack onto the deck of the boat and into its small cabin, which held a ratty couch. How ironic that they had started their day planning to escape from a boat, only to end up in another one.

She helped Jack out of his wet clothes, stripping him of his shirt, pants, socks, and shoes, and covered him with one of the thin ragged bath towels she'd found in the hold. "Sorry. I know it's not great, but it's all we got."

She rummaged around for supplies, finding a small

kerosene lamp in the galley kitchen. She lit the lamp, wishing it would give out more light, or at least more heat. Inside, the boat was almost as cold as it was outside.

"Are you comfortable?" she asked.

He nodded, still unable to speak, either in words or in her mind.

She turned her back and peeled off her own wet things, feeling shy around him, and wrapped herself in a towel as well. The nautical shower was working, probably left with a few gallons of water from its last trip, and she was glad for the opportunity to wash after such a long day. She was also thankful the boat contained a few dry clothes for them to change into: sailor shirts, swim shorts. They would have to do.

After she showered and dressed, Schuyler then helped Jack walk down the few steps into the small bathroom, closing the door behind him.

Thunder rumbled in the distance. It would rain again soon. The wind howled, lashing against the portholes. Schuyler made sure the latch on the cabin door was secure.

When Jack limped out of the shower, Schuyler was glad to see that he looked a little better. The color had returned to his cheeks. He picked up a blanket from the couch and threw it over his shoulders. "Come here," he whispered, opening his arms so that she could huddle against him, her back against his chest. She could feel his body begin to thaw, and she pulled his arms around her tightly, massaging his hands until they were warm again.

In a soft voice, Jack told her what had happened to him. He had stayed a beat longer on the boat to give Schuyler a head start, and had guided it straight at the Jet Skis. But the Venators had taken that as an opportunity to jump on board, and he had fought them off. One of them had gotten away—the woman who had come after Schuyler. The other one had been a fight to the death.

"What do you mean?" Schuyler asked.

"He had a black sword with him," Jack said slowly, raising a hand to the fire and making the flame leap. "I had to use it. It was him or me." He looked so anguished, Schuyler put a protective hand on his shoulder. Jack bowed his head. "Tabris. I knew him. He was a friend of mine. A long time ago."

Jack had called the Venator by his angel name. Schuyler sucked in her breath. She felt guilty for everything—all this killing—it was all her fault. She had been the one who convinced Jack they should seek refuge with the Countess. She was the one who had brought them to Europe. This quest was her legacy, not his—her responsibility she'd latched on his shoulders. She was the one who had planned their escape—no one was supposed to be hurt. She hadn't realized that the Countess would take it so far—the black sword— dear God. If Jack had not bested the Venator, then he would be the one whose immortal life was finished.

He drew her closer to him and whispered fiercely in

her ear. "It had to be done. I gave him a choice. He chose death. Death will come to all, sooner or later." Jack pressed his head against hers, and she could feel the veins throbbing below his skin.

Death will come to all? Jack of all people should know that wasn't true. The Blue Bloods had survived for centuries. Schuyler wondered if he was thinking of Mimi—Azrael— just then. *Death will come to all.* Would it come to Jack? Would Mimi exercise her right to a burning and extinguish Jack's spirit forever?

Schuyler wasn't as concerned about her own mortality as she was for his. If he died, there would be no life for her. Please, God, no. Not yet. Give us this time still. This small sliver of time that we have together, let it last as long as it can.

FIVE

Breaking Bread

*S*chuyler had fallen asleep in Jack's arms, but she woke up, blinking her eyes, when she heard a rustling noise. The fire in the lamp was still flickering, but the rain had stopped. The only sound was the lapping of waves against the hull. Jack placed a finger to his lips. *Quiet. Someone's here.*

"*Signorina?*" A dark figure hovered by the doorway.

Before Schuyler could answer, Jack had sprung from his seat and held Ghedi by the throat.

"Jack! Wait, what are you doing? It's Ghedi—he helped me! He was the one who got me out of the water, Jack! Let him go!"

Ghedi's dark face had turned several shades of gray. He was holding a basket in his hands, which was now shaking slightly.

"Bossing . . ." he protested. "I bring food. Bread. Dinner."

"You serve us well, human," Jack said coldly. "Maybe too well. Tell us, who do you truly serve?"

Schuyler felt indignation burn her cheeks. "Jack, please! You're being ridiculous!"

"Only if he tells me who he really is and who he's working for. A Somali pirate wouldn't give a rat's ass about two American kids, especially once he was paid. Why did you follow us? Are you a servant of the Countess?"

Ghedi shook his head, and looked them straight in the eye. "Have no fear, my friends, for I am a friend of the professor."

Schuyler was surprised to hear the Somali speaking perfect English, and no longer with the African intonations he'd affected before.

"The professor?" Jack asked, relaxing his grip slightly.

"Professor Lawrence Van Alen, of course."

"You knew my grandfather?" Schuyler asked. "Why didn't you mention it earlier? At the market?"

Ghedi did not reply. Instead, he reached into the basket and brought out sacks of flour, salt, and a small jar of sardines. "First we must eat. I know you do not need it for sustenance, but please, for the sake of companionship, let us share a meal before we discuss."

"Hold on," Jack said. "You speak the names of our friends, yet how do we know you are truly a friend to us? Lawrence Van Alen had as many enemies as allies."

"All you say is true. Yet there is nothing I can show or say that will prove I am who I say I am. You will have to decide for yourself whether I am telling the truth. I have no mark, no papers, nothing that may attest to my story. You have only my word. You must trust your own judgment."

Jack looked at Schuyler. *What do you think?*

I don't know. You're right to be cautious. But I feel in my heart he is a friend. But that is all I have. A feeling.

Instincts are all we have in the end. Instincts and luck, Jack sent.

Jack said, "We will trust you tonight, Ghedi. You're right, you must eat, as must she. Please . . ." He released his hold and motioned to the fire.

Ghedi whistled while he pounded out the injera dough into small circles in the small galley kitchen. He found a metal skillet and fired up one of the gas burners. With the other, he grilled a few sardines on an open flame. In a few minutes, the bread began to rise, puffing with small indentations. The fish began to smoke. When it was ready, Ghedi prepared three plates.

The bread was a bit sour and spongy, but Schuyler thought it was the best thing she had ever eaten. She didn't even realize until she smelled the fresh, delicious aroma filling the room that she was hungry. Starving even. The fish was excellent, and along with a few fresh tomatoes Ghedi had unearthed, it made a satisfying meal. Jack had a piece or two, to be polite. But Schuyler and Ghedi ate as if it was their last meal.

So it wasn't a coincidence, then, their meeting Ghedi at the market, Schuyler thought, appraising their new companion as she dipped a piece of bread into the small pool of ghee on her plate. When she thought about it a little more, she remembered that it was the pirate who had approached them. And now, on further recollection, it seemed that he was waiting for them. He had practically ambushed them when they had walked past his stall, asking if there was any way he could be of service. He had been quite persuasive, and somehow Schuyler had managed to communicate the specifics of their confinement, and they had finally agreed to trust him with getting them a motorboat.

But who *was* Ghedi after all? How did he know Lawrence?

"I know you have many questions," the Somali said. "But it is late. And we must all rest. Tomorrow, I will return and tell you what I know."

Six

Motherless Boys

"I was six years old when they took my mother," Ghedi told them the following morning with their breakfasts—cups of espresso and fresh bread in a brown paper bag.

Schuyler raised her eyebrows while Jack looked grim. They sipped their coffee and listened. Outside, the seagulls were greeting the dawn with their mournful screeching. Fishing season was over, so there was no worry of the boat's owner finding them, but they wanted to move on as early as possible.

"The raiders had never come so close to the coast before, but we had heard about them from neighboring villages. They always took the womenfolk—young girls, usually." Ghedi shrugged his shoulders as if to apologize. "I was told my mother was getting water by the creek when they took her. She was very beautiful, my mother. When she came back, she was different." Ghedi shook his head, a hard light in his eyes. "She was . . . changed. And her belly, swollen."

"She had been raped, then?" Schuyler asked gently.

"Yes and no . . . She did not remember any violence. She did not remember anything, really. My father had died in the wars, a year before, and when the baby came, it took her life with his. Neither survived. I was the only one left. My uncle took me to the missionaries. They ran an orphanage in Berbera. It was full of lost boys like me—war orphans, motherless boys.

"One day Father Baldessarre came."

"Baldessarre, did you say?" Schuyler asked, looking startled. "How did you know him? We are looking for him as well." When she had left New York she'd taken Lawrence's notes with her. The papers that she carried from his files named a Father Baldessarre in conjunction with the Gate of Promise, and finding the priest seemed a good place to start their own journey.

Ghedi explained. "Father Baldessarre was the head of the Petruvian mission. He was very kind, and he chose several boys to take back to Italy, to send to their school in Florence. I was one of them. At first I did not want to leave. I was scared. But I liked going to school. And I liked Father B. He taught us to speak English and sent most of the boys to new lives in America. I thought that was where I would end up as well. Somewhere in Kansas. Going to community college." He smiled ruefully and rubbed his shaved head.

"One day after class, Father B. pulled me aside. I was eleven years old—old enough, he decided, to help them with their true mission. He told me he was entrusted with a powerful secret. The Petruvian Order was not an ordinary brotherhood; they were guardians of a sacred space.

"Two years ago, when I had formally joined the order and was ordained as a priest, Father B. received a letter from a Professor Lawrence Van Alen, requesting a visit. The professor seemed to know many things about our work, and Father B. believed the professor would be able to help with our mission. Certain things had begun to happen that could not be explained, dark omens that worried him. We prepared for this meeting, but the professor never arrived, and Father B. began to get agitated. He began to worry. He was ill, Father B.; he had been diagnosed with cancer the year before and he knew he didn't have much time. And then last year, out of the blue, Christopher Anderson came to visit us.

"He told us the Professor was dead, but his legacy lived on in his granddaughter, and that she would help us with our task. He showed us your photograph, Schuyler. He told us to keep an eye out for you, to help you when you came into our region. We have been waiting for you since, especially when we heard you had left New York. Of course, we had no idea that you were in the custody of the Countess. That we did not count on."

Ghedi wiped his brow with a handkerchief. "Father B. could not wait any longer. The wrongness was growing, he said. He told me to come find you instead, and to bring you back to our monastery. I apologize for not identifying myself sooner, but I was wary of approaching you as a Petruvian until you were safely away from your imprisonment."

"Where is Father B. now?" Schuyler asked.

At this, Ghedi's face changed again. Now it looked weary. "I am sorry to tell you, Father has passed away."

"When?" Schuyler looked stricken. So close, but always a dead end—literally—when they got there. Jack continued to look at Ghedi keenly, never taking his eyes away from their new friend's face.

"Two weeks ago, on one of the missions to Africa, they were all taken—slaughtered by raiders. I escaped by joining the Somali Marines for a short while. Don't worry—I'm a priest, not a pirate. The minute I was able to get back to Europe I resumed my search for you."

"You've found her," Jack said sharply. "So what now?"

"You're going to take us to the Gate of Promise, aren't you, Ghedi?" Schuyler asked, throwing her cup in the trash, marveling that Lawrence's instincts had been right as usual. "With Father Baldessarre gone . . ."

"I am the gatekeeper." Ghedi nodded. "And I will take you to Florence. That is where you are headed, yes?"

Seven

The Trail

*S*chuyler estimated that at *Velox* speed, it would take them a little over a week to get to Florence, a hundred miles away. Since Ghedi could not keep up, he would accompany them only until Sarzana, then take the train to Florence to prepare for their arrival and meet them in town. Meanwhile, Jack decided they would stay off the main road, and use the mountain footpaths instead. It was safer that way; the hills were rocky and remote at this time of year. Less chance of bumping into one of the Countess's spies or henchmen. Since it was illegal to camp in the mountains, they would have to be extra careful to avoid other hikers or park rangers.

Nothing more had been said about Ghedi's surprising announcement, as the logistics of their trip took all of their attention. But even as she went through the motions of packing, Schuyler continued to mull about the turn of events, how quickly it had all come together. As much as they had been searching for him, the gatekeeper had been searching for them. It seemed almost too easy.

Most unsettling of all, however, was something neither she nor Jack had yet to address. Ghedi professed to be the gatekeeper. There was just one hitch. Ghedi was human. There was no way he could be who he said he was. It was impossible, as only a Blue Blood vampire, a fallen angel, could guard one of the Gates of Hell.

Yet I do not think he is lying, Schuyler sent.

I agree. He believes he is the gatekeeper, which is more troubling, Jack replied. *Let's deal with this later. For now, we must leave this place as quickly as we can.*

The three of them went into town to load up on supplies, purchasing only things they could carry on their backs and nothing they didn't need. Before leaving New York, Jack had transferred monies to several secret offshore accounts that remained unknown to the Committee. He left to find suitable outdoor equipment while Schuyler and Ghedi went to the market to buy food—more flour, rice, coffee, eggs, canned soups. The Italian proprietress regarded Ghedi's dark skin and Schuyler's odd clothes with a suspicious eye, but she was mollified when Schuyler pulled out a huge bankroll of euros.

Schuyler wondered about her newfound appetite. She was voracious, and it was a hunger that could be satisfied with a good meal. She had not taken the blood since leaving New York. Jack had urged her to perform the *Caerimonia*

Osculor, but she found there was no need. If anything, she felt stronger and more clearheaded without the blood. She strove to avoid it for as long as she was able. It felt wrong, somehow, to share something so intimate with someone who wasn't her love. With Oliver, of course, it had been different. It was still difficult to think about her best friend and former familiar. Her heart had healed, but she missed their friendship.

"I am sorry about your mother, Ghedi," Schuyler said as they walked back to meet Jack at the boat. "We both are."

"It is all right. She is dead now. It is better."

"Don't say that."

"It is the truth. Now she is at peace."

"And Father B., too," Schuyler added. "You must have been very close to him."

"He was the only family I ever really knew. He taught me everything. But it is all right, *signorina*. In my country I have seen worse. I was very lucky to have been chosen by the missionaries." Ghedi smiled.

It was amazing how someone who had survived the double-fisted tragedy of war and grief could call himself lucky, Schuyler thought. Whether he was telling them the truth or was simply confused or misinformed about what or who he was, he was a good man, she could feel it. She found much to admire in Ghedi's humor and optimism, and chastised herself for her constant anxiety and stress. Ghedi had lost everything, not once but several times in his life. His home was a pile of rubble, his entire family was dead, and his mentor murdered. Yet he treaded lightly, with a spring in his step and a smile on his face.

Whereas she who had everything—for Jack was everything—was constantly bemoaning the fact that she had no idea how long it would last, the two of them together. Instead of fearing the future, I should live and enjoy the present, she told herself.

When they arrived back at the harbor, Jack was locking up the cabin. He had folded the blankets, refilled the kerosene lamp, and had made sure the fishing boat was no worse for wear after their visit.

Thank you for sheltering us, Schuyler thought, putting a hand on a cabin wall. May your harvests be plentiful. She picked up one of the hiker's racks that Jack had left on the deck and began to fill it with provisions: the food supplies, a thin waterproof blanket, the battered Repository files that she kept in a watertight envelope.

Schuyler lifted her pack onto her shoulders and struggled a bit under the weight until she found her bearings.

"Too heavy?" Jack asked. "I can take more." He was already carrying the tents and the bulk of their supplies.

"No, it's all right."

Ghedi straightened up as well. "Ready?"

They kept to the paved road that led from the town up to the mountain path, which was mostly deserted except for an occasional car or two. Once they were a few miles out of town, Jack led them off the road, deeper into the forest. Schuyler was glad for the new warm jacket she had bought in town, along with the thick socks and the hiking boots. For a while she marveled at how much her life had changed.

How odd to think that not too long ago she was sitting in a classroom dreaming her life away, lost in a world of her own making, living as if she were almost half asleep, a wallflower on the fringes, the girl without a voice. Then last year, she and Oliver had embarked on that harried, whirlwind tour around the world—their only instinct to run away as far and fast as they could. She realized that was why there had been so many close brushes with the Venators, who patrolled the metropolitan areas. She and Oliver had been on their turf.

But not in the forests, Jack had explained. Not in the wild. Here, they were safe.

For fifteen years Schuyler had almost never left New York. What a difference the Transformation had made; not only had she traveled all round the globe, now she was hiking the Italian mountain range. She looked over to Jack, who felt her gaze.

All right? he sent.

"It's an adventure." She smiled. It was a rush being on their own, finally free of the Countess. *Every day with you is a new adventure.*

Jack smiled and continued to forge ahead, clearing a

path with his walking stick, brushing away dead branches and warning them of slippery rocks.

For a human, Ghedi displayed a monumental level of endurance, but even he was tired after a full day's climb. They arrived at a plateau near the top of Monte Rosa and stopped to enjoy the panoramic view of the coast below. They had made good time. Tomorrow, if they kept up the pace, they would be in Pontremoli by midnight.

They agreed to rest for the evening. There was a creek not too far away where they could refill their water bottles, and the ground was nice and dry. Ghedi chose to set up a little ways away to give them their privacy. Schuyler removed her pack and helped Jack set up their tent. They worked wordlessly together, a team. Once the tent was secure, Schuyler offered to bring fresh water to boil for supper. She poured the water into the kettle and set it on the fire that Jack had started.

"We have to ask him," Schuyler said, kneeling in front of the flames. "It just doesn't make sense, unless he was Baldessarre's Conduit. But somehow I don't think he was."

Jack promised to bring it up, and when Ghedi joined them in front of the fire, Jack let their friend warm up a little before he asked the question. "Tell me, Ghedi," he said in a friendly voice. "How is it that one of the most important places in our history has come under the jurisdiction of a teenage priest?" Jack removed his shoe and shook out a few pebbles, stretching his long legs closer to the fire. He had adopted a casual air, but for a moment Schuyler was worried Jack was going to grab Ghedi by the throat again.

"What happened to the vampires who were guarding the site, you mean," Ghedi said. He gazed off into the distance. "They are lost."

"Killed?"

"I do not know. No one does. They have been gone a long time now. Father B. told me that when his order took over, only the Conduits were left. The original guardians were long gone."

"Silver Bloods?" Schuyler asked, looking at Jack.

"No." Jack shook his head. "If the Croatan had taken the gate, the world as we know it would not exist. Something else must have happened."

"You mentioned that Father B. had questions for Lawrence," she said to Ghedi. "I don't know if I have those answers, but I can try to find them. That's what we're here for."

"Yes. We have much to discuss, but it is a dangerous business. Let us talk when we are in the safety of the monastery. The original gatekeepers put wards there." He looked nervously around the surrounding woods, scared that they were being watched. Schuyler understood that even in their relative isolation, with the Silver Blood threat, one was never quite alone.

"Ghedi is right: we shall not mention it until then," Jack

said, throwing a stick into the fire and watching the flames dance around it.

Schuyler agreed, Ghedi's words turning over slowly in her head. Something about what he'd said was bothering her. *When the Petruvian Order took over, only the Conduits were left.* "So Father Baldessarre, he wasn't . . . he wasn't a vampire either," she said slowly, letting the information sink in. She still couldn't believe it.

"No. He was human, like me."

"And when did his order take charge?" Jack asked sharply.

"Sometime in the fifteenth century."

Schuyler exchanged a wary look with Jack. Humans had been in charge of protecting one of the Gates of Hell for centuries now. This was certainly not what they had thought they would find on their search. Human gatekeepers! What did this mean? And what questions did they have? What were they hoping her grandfather would tell them?

Ghedi said good night, and retired for the evening. When he was gone, Schuyler removed the stack of Repository files from her pack. She rifled through the yellowed pages, reading.

"I just don't understand," she said, looking up from her papers. "Halcyon was an Enmortal. Like Lawrence, like Kingsley, like every one of those who were inducted into the Order of the Seven. So how did Father Baldessarre and the Petruvians come to be the gatekeepers? Something must have happened in the fifteenth century—but what?"

Jack frowned. "The only reason would be desperation. Halcyon must have had no other choice. Otherwise, why would she trust a group of humans to do a vampire's job?"

They puzzled over it some more. Schuyler did not want to voice any more fears or show how unsettled their latest discovery had made her. While she was half-human herself, the Blue Bloods were strictly a closed society. Human knowledge of vampire existence was tightly restricted to the traditional positions of familiar or Conduit. Red Bloods were not privy to the workings of the shadow world. What Ghedi had described was a breach of the highest level, something that could upend everything she knew and understood about the Code of the Vampires. And if the Code was not real, then what was?

She took the first watch and kissed Jack good night. He could not argue her out of it, and had finally agreed to rest.

Schuyler shivered slightly, but something told her it wasn't from the mountain breeze. Four centuries had past with *human* gatekeepers guarding the Gate of Promise. She was glad for the fire. It burned a clear, azure blue, steady and true, against the wind.

The Man from the Citadel

The Silver Blood chanced a glance in their direction, and immediately the cloaked stranger disappeared.

"We've been spotted. Now!" Dre urged, running toward their prey. Gio and Tomi burst out of the shadows, golden swords at the ready, and the chase resumed.

They followed the Silver Blood through the crooked streets, all the way into the cathedral, to the very top of Brunelleschi's unfinished dome, the highest point in Florence.

The Silver Blood dodged their blows with an agility and strength equal to their own. It was unlike any other they had ever encountered, but in the end, it was still no match for the three armed Venators. Backed into a corner, it snarled and hissed, knowing it had already lost.

Dre drew his sword to its throat and prepared to deliver the final stroke, when a voice rang out from the stairway. Someone else had followed them up to the spire.

"Heel, Venator."

They turned to see a hooded stranger approach. Under the moonlight, they saw that he was wearing the colored robes and gold chains of the Citadel. His features were still hidden by the hood of his cloak, but it was the same human the Silver Blood had spoken to earlier.

"This creature is not yours to send to Hell, for he is already there," the dark man declared, and with a wave of his hand the Silver Blood disappeared into the black flames.

Tomi gasped, shocked and dismayed as she realized that the creature they were chasing was no Silver Blood, no fallen angel from Heaven, but a demon from Hell itself.

The hooded stranger teetered on the edge of the rim. He lifted a single foot outward into nothingness and plunged through the chasm of the unfinished dome. His robes blown wide in the wind revealed three black symbols engraved in the flesh of his arm. One was of a sword piercing a star. The last time she'd seen that symbol was on Lucifer's wrist in Rome, when the Dark Prince of the Silver Bloods was calling himself Caligula.

The three Venators ran down to the bottom of the church, where they found the body of the hooded stranger carrying Lucifer's mark.

The Red Blood was dead.

Eight

Wildflowers

Even though the sunlight, lovely and warm, was streaming into the tent, when Schuyler woke up, she felt a fearsome cold. She had gotten so used to sleeping next to Jack's warm body, she was at a bit of a loss to find that he was not by her side. She groped at the emptiness next to her. His sleeping bag was still warm. He had not been gone long.

Love? she sent.

I am near, do not worry. Go back to sleep.

She laid her head back against the blankets and fell asleep, dreaming of fields strewn with wildflowers.

An hour later she rose and walked down to the nearby creek they had found the night before. All her life she had lived in relative comfort, and it was strange to be out in the wild, to feel unencumbered and liberated from the routine of modern life.

She took off her shirt and her waterlogged shoes, stripped

down to her underwear. She would wash her clothes in the stream. In the absence of soap, she hit the fabric with a rock to shake out the dirt. This much she knew from watching Hattie wash the clothes at home. Cordelia had not thought much of modern appliances.

She was in the middle of her chore when she felt a presence behind her. She turned to see Jack watching her. He smiled, the first real smile she'd seen on his face since they had left New York. It had been difficult to fully enjoy each other's company under the watchful gaze of the Countess's Venators.

"Good morning." She smiled. Jack had washed as well, and his hair was shiny in the sun. He was as handsome as a god, she thought. Was it just her imagination, or had their exile and journey added to his visage? Every day he looked less like the pretty-boy lacrosse player he had been, and more like the ancient heavenly warrior he really was.

"I brought you something," he said, holding out a bouquet of tiny violet sprays.

She put one in her hair. Even in the midst of everything they were doing, he was always thinking of her. "Thank you."

He put his arms around her, and soon they were lying in the grass together. She slipped her hands under his shirt, loving how warm and strong his body felt against hers, loving how closely he held her. Yet even though they were together, she could not stop worrying about how much time they would have—

We have all the time in the world.

You don't know that. What if . . . She hated how worried she sounded, but she couldn't help it.

Don't. Whatever happens, happens.

Right.

They were prepared to face whatever consequences breaking the bond would bring. Mimi's wrath. The wasting disease that would weaken him to the point of paralysis. They were up to the challenge.

But I'm scared, she sent.

I'm not.

In a way, their monthlong incarceration had been useful, as they had been able to articulate their fears and hopes for the future, testing the boundaries of their new relationship. They had been able to plan not only for the immediate situation, but for whatever dark destiny awaited them. Schuyler knew where she stood with Jack. And he knew where she was coming from. She had never felt more secure or certain about anything in her life than the depth and fortitude of his love. He had gone to Hell and back to save her, and she had given her blood to him to save his life.

But the bond . . .

We shall forge a new bond.

You don't have doubts about relinquishing the old? Schuyler had never felt brave enough to ask him this question before, as she still feared his answer. She had never used their closeness in the glom to peer into his memories, to see if he had any regrets for the choice he had made. She respected his privacy, but she also knew she would not be able to bear it if she found that he carried a lingering yearning for his twin. She would die of jealousy to know it.

Not one. This is a bond we choose to make, not one that was decided for us. I don't believe in fate. I don't believe that love is predetermined.

"We should get back," Schuyler whispered. They didn't have time for this. No time for love; for each other.

"Not yet," Jack sighed, his eyes still closed, his warm fingers tracing a line down her naked stomach.

Schuyler smiled at him indulgently, letting her hair brush his cheek. He twined a fistful and pulled her to him so that their lips met again. She opened her mouth to his, and his hand reached underneath her camisole.

She bent down toward him, straddling his waist, then he flipped her over so that she lay supine underneath him, her white throat open and exposed.

He traced a finger on her neck, and she closed her eyes in anticipation.

She could feel him kiss her jaw, then underneath her neck, and she pulled him closer, closer.

Finally he let his teeth slide over her skin, and then in one quick thrust, she felt his fangs pierce her.

She gasped. It was the strongest he had ever dared, the deepest intrusion into her body, and one she had not been ready for, but it was glorious. She could feel his very life force intermingling with hers, could feel the beat of his heart in her heart—the two of them together, as he held her in his grasp. She felt light-headed and dizzy and drugged, and her arms clutched his back as she pulled him ever closer, ever nearer.

More, she thought. *More*.

In answer, Jack released her for a moment, then bit her a second time. This time, when he kissed her with his fangs, the piercing sweetness filled her with that same painful but wonderful ache.

She was his love and his familiar. They were attached in a thousand ways—tiny invisible hooks that bound them to each other no matter what Heaven or its former residents declared.

NINE

Ambush

By the time Schuyler heard the sound of footsteps it was almost midday. The group coming upon her and Jack thought they could take them by surprise, but in that they were wrong. She kept her eyes closed and her head on Jack's chest. She had heard them from several hundred feet away, the crunching of twigs underfoot, their stealthy step across the forest floor, their hushed conversations.

Don't move, Jack sent. *Let's see what they want.*

Schuyler was not afraid, yet she was worried. The group coming upon them were not Venators, but she could smell their desperation and fear, and knew that they did not mean them well. What were she and Jack thinking, anyway, taking a languid morning for themselves? Thank goodness they had put their clothes back on.

She could feel Jack breathing underneath her, could hear his steady heartbeat.

"Get up," a gruff voice ordered.

Schuyler yawned and stretched and pretended to blink her eyes. She rose and looked around. Jack followed her lead. With their tousled hair and red cheeks, they looked like two young people who had been roused from a nap.

They were surrounded by a group of men carrying rifles and handguns. From their bearing and their speech, Schuyler guessed they were peasants from a neighboring town, probably from Santo Stefano, which was the nearest. The countryside was filled with folk who had never left the villages, who carried on the traditions and trades taught and handed down for generations. The modern world had brought them cell phones and Internet cafés, yet they lived in several-hundred-year-old farmhouses with no heating, and continued to make their bread and sausages by hand.

The men pointed their guns and stared. These were not evil men, Schuyler realized. They were frightened and spooked, but they were not evil. She exhaled a little.

Jack raised his arms. "We do not mean you any harm," he said in perfect Italian.

"It is illegal to camp in the mountains. Who are you and where do you come from?" demanded a lean man with narrowed eyes.

"We are Americans. We are from New York . . . on a backpacking trip," Schuyler answered, appealing to their sense of hospitality. The Italians loved American tourists. More dollars to buy their overpriced gelato.

Another man wearing a Fiat T-shirt and cocking an old-fashioned Beretta pistol nodded. "We do not like strangers here."

"We are just passing through; we did not realize it was wrong to camp here," Schuyler explained. "Please . . . just let us go and we will be on our way."

Jack made to stand, but found a gun pointed at his head.

"Stay where you are."

"Please be reasonable," Jack said mildly, but there was an edge to his tone.

"Shut up."

Schuyler glanced at Jack. If he wanted to, in an instant he could obliterate all of them from the landscape.

Don't, she told him.

She closed her eyes and concentrated. She could hear their thoughts in the glom.

They're just kids, we should let them go, what is Gino thinking. They can't have gone too far with MariElena, we are wasting time. They might know something. What will we do with them now? This is stupid. We should go. Leave them alone. Hold them until they talk. Strange times. Strangers. Strange. No we cannot trust.

They need our help, Schuyler realized. They were frightened and confused, and in the middle of their fear was a girl. No. They feared *for* the girl. She could see the girl clearly in their subconscious—a young girl, just a year or two younger than she was. Schuyler made a decision. "Please. Tell us what has happened," she said. "We might be able to help you. You are looking for someone, yes? Someone who is dear to all of you. We are friends of Father Baldessarre."

At the mention of the priest's name, the group relaxed. Schuyler had guessed as much. The Petruvian Order meant something around these parts. Father Baldessarre was a holy man, a respected man, a man whose name carried a lot of weight. A lot of credibility. She was reminded, achingly, of her grandfather.

"Let us help you," Schuyler said. "We are . . . trained to do so. Please, tell us what's happened."

The men glanced at each other, then finally the oldest one spoke. "They took my daughter, MariElena," the big man said, then could not go on any longer, for he had put his hands to his face and begun to sob.

Luca, the youngest of the group, explained. His father and brothers and uncles were looking for MariElena, his sister, who had been abducted last night by smugglers from the flesh trade—a danger not unknown in this part of the world. He handed Schuyler a photograph of a pretty, dark-haired girl, with thick eyebrows and a shy smile. Fifteen years old. "Mostly they take girls from the small villages in Eastern Europe, but now they are more daring. They have come to our part of the world. Life is not difficult here, as you can see," he said, motioning to the verdant Italian countryside. "But it is boring, it is the same, it lacks excitement.

"Mari met him at the Internet café. He was Russian, but he told her he was going to school in America. She called him her boyfriend. They 'eloped' last night, but we don't think they are getting married." He showed them his cell phone. "I got this a few hours ago." There was a text message from MariElena. It read *Aiuto*—Italian for *help*.

"We are very sorry to hear about your sister. But why not go to the police?" Jack wanted to know.

"Because they are paid off by the smugglers—as usual," Luca explained. "But we think they are not far, for they would not have taken the roads—so they must still be here in the mountains. Most likely they are headed to Levanto, where the freighters dock."

"What will happen to her if you don't find her?" Schuyler asked, although she knew the answer.

Luca frowned. "The same thing that happens to all these girls. She'll be sold and taken away. Then we'll never see her again."

TEN

Hidden

chuyler led the group back to their campsite, where they found Ghedi waiting for them with their bags packed. When he heard about the girl's abduction he grew agitated. He took Schuyler aside while Jack organized the men into search parties.

"This kidnapping—I need to talk to you about it. MariElena is only the latest to be taken," he said as he contrived to hide their bags in the bushes.

"Yes, they told us that. That girls from this region have gone missing," she said as she helped pile rocks on their folded tents. They would return for them later.

"No, it is more than that." Ghedi looked frustrated. "It is not safe for me to speak of it here. I wanted to wait until we were well protected. But I need to tell you."

"Yes?"

Ghedi looked at his watch. "She was taken last night.

That is too long. It is too late already. They should have come to the monastery the minute she was missing. The others might have been able to find her before . . ." He shook his head. "Instead they set off themselves. In doing so they sealed her fate."

"I don't understand," Schuyler said. "Whatever happens to her, we have to try and find her. We have to try and save her."

The young priest shook his head and would not say any more, promising to explain when they reached the monastery and leaving Schuyler to puzzle over his words.

Jack had split the company into two groups. One half would head farther up the mountains while the other half made for the port. Ghedi accompanied the second group; he was familiar with the workings of shipyards and would be able to sniff out those who traded in illegal human cargo. Schuyler and Jack would take their own path and keep in contact with the rest with a walkie-talkie loaned from Luca.

When the team disbanded, Schuyler told Jack what Ghedi had said. Jack agreed there was no way they were going to abandon the girl, no matter what Ghedi was worried about. As a sworn Venator, Jack was charged with not only serving the Coven but protecting the innocent—whether vampire or human. He suggested they waste no time on a footrace. The fastest way to find the girl was to locate her spirit in the glom.

"It is better if you do it—she might not hide from you,"

he said, explaining that a gentle female presence would be more successful at coaxing a young girl from her hiding place.

Schuyler closed her eyes and reached out into the darkness. She concentrated on the image from the photograph.

MariElena, where are you?

When Schuyler opened her eyes, she was standing in the twilight world of the glom. She could sense Jack's presence as well as the spirits of the company searching for the girl. The glom world was silvery and dim, veiled as if by a dense gray fog.

MariElena, I am a friend. Show yourself. You are safe with me. Tell me where you are. Your family is looking for you.

There was no answer.

Schuyler waited, but it was as if she were calling down into a bottomless well. She could sense her consciousness expanding beyond the universe, but there was nothing to push back against it—the sign that she had located the right spirit. She opened her eyes.

"Nothing?" Jack asked.

"Not a thing." Schuyler frowned. "It's like she's not here . . . not even in the glom. Not like she's hiding. More like . . . she never existed." She swallowed her frustration. Ghedi's warning had unsettled her. What was the gatekeeper so afraid of?

More than anything, Schuyler wanted to bring MariElena safely home. She felt a kinship with the young girl. Wasn't she herself just fifteen when her life changed? She understood how MariElena might fall in love with a stranger, how one might be tempted by curiosity and adventure, how terrible to have that curiosity of the world shattered so horribly.

I am here! Help me! Help me!

"Oh God," Schuyler said. "I just heard her."

Help me. Help. Kill. Help. Die. Help. Fire. Help. Hell. Help. The girl's thoughts were an incoherent, frightened plea, a monologue of confused desperation.

Schuyler reached out to Jack, who steadied her. *You are safe, you are safe, you are safe now. Show me where you are. We will find you and bring you to safety*, she sent, projecting a soothing calmness to the shattered soul.

Help me. Help me. Help me. Kill. Die. Help. Fire. Help. Hell. Help.

Schuyler jerked awake. She opened her eyes.

"You found her?" Jack asked. He was still holding her tightly.

"Yes. I know where she is." Schuyler picked up the walkie-talkie and described what she saw to the rest of the searchers. A dark cavern by a dry riverbed, a gaping hole in the ground, overhung with moss.

There was a startled cry from Ghedi on the receiving end.

"What's wrong?" she asked. "Where is she?"

"The cavern by the dry river. It's called Hellsmouth," he said, his voice rising in panic. "A few miles outside of Florence. I'll meet you there."

Schuyler understood Ghedi's reaction immediately. Maybe this was why the priest had been so pessimistic about MariElena's chances.

"They've taken her to the gate," she told Jack. "Come on, we don't have much time."

ELEVEN

Hellsmouth

hedi gave them precise directions, and Jack and Schuyler set off immediately, their *Velox* speed taking them to their destination in a flash of butterfly wings.

If they were taking her to the gate, then they weren't smugglers, Schuyler thought. And if they weren't smugglers, then what were they? What did they want with the girl? Was this what the priest was worried about? What Ghedi had not wanted to tell them until they were "safe"?

They found the dried riverbed, a scarlet, sandy ribbon of patched, scorched earth that led to a dark underground cavern. Just as Schuyler had described, the cavern was covered in moss and half sunken into the earth.

Jack kicked away at the shrubbery blocking the entrance and led the way down. He picked up a stick and lit it with the blue flame.

"Show yourselves!" he called, his voice echoing against the stone walls.

The cave was dark and smelled of mold. Was this the entrance to the Gate of Promise? Schuyler could feel a foul, putrid menace in the air as they inched their way down, taking careful steps into the murky blackness.

"Hellsmouth. Interesting name, isn't it? The Red Bloods seem to have a knack for naming things without knowing their true significance. But obviously they sensed something here," she said.

"No one is immune to the feeling of power," he replied, his torch sending long rays of light down a seemingly endless tunnel.

Schuyler slipped a little on the wet moss, grabbing on to Jack's arm for balance. She looked around the dark enclosure. Down there, she was surprised to find that the heavy feeling of doom had abated somewhat, replaced by a lonesome melancholy. She walked forward in the darkness, and the feeling grew stronger.

They stopped and looked around the shadowy space, Jack's torch illuminating a rather standard-looking cavern, with moss green rocks and a sandy floor. The cave was littered with the usual teenage detritus: crushed cigarette butts and empty beer bottles.

Something isn't right, Jack sent.

You feel it too? Schuyler asked. *What is it?*

Then she knew. *It's not here, is it? This isn't the Gate of Promise.*

No, this is a mere vapor, a distraction. A cunning illusion.

Hellsmouth was nothing but a haunted house, something to scare away the local populace, a distraction from the real menace.

"What do we know about Blue Bloods?" Jack mused.

"That they don't like to make anything easy?" Schuyler said. "That they keep their secrets. They brought peace and art and light to the world. They are a highly civilized people. They built temples and monuments, cities of gold that rise to the heavens," she said, thinking of Paris and how beautiful it was.

"Exactly. Think of the gates we've already found—the Gate of Vengeance under a statue—a sculpture, an icon. The second underneath one of the most beautiful Gothic cathedrals in North America. A vampire would not build a gate in a hole in the ground, a crude cavern in the sand." Jack shook his head.

"No. You're absolutely right. Whoever put this here did so to conceal the gate's true location." Schuyler said. "But if this isn't the gate—then why are the Petruvians guarding it?"

TWELVE

The Symbol

*S*chuyler paced the rocky floor. How much did they know about the Petruvian Order after all? That first night, Ghedi had asked them to trust him—he had named Lawrence Van Alen as a friend, yet he had never met the man. How much of his story was true? After their month of imprisonment as guests of the Countess, Schuyler chided herself for not being more careful.

"Do you think we might've been wrong about Ghedi?" she asked Jack.

He shook his head. "It is better to trust and face betrayal than to remain skeptical of everything and everybody. Your open heart is a gift. It led you to me, for instance.

"But in this case I don't believe Ghedi played us. The Croatan have no use for Red Bloods. I doubt he has ever set foot in here. If, as I'm guessing, the Petruvian Order was founded by the original gatekeeper, Halcyon would have followed a certain standard for dealing with humans. It's common practice, the Conspiracy has done it for hundreds of years. They tell the Red Bloods only as much as they need to know."

They took one more sweep around the dark cavern, and Schuyler noticed something they hadn't seen before, a symbol etched on one of the walls. It was a triglyph, a symbol in three parts. The first consisted of two interlocking circles, the Blue Bloods' symbol for union; the second was of an animal they couldn't identify. The third symbol was one Schuyler had never seen before: a sword piercing a star.

"It's the archangel's sigil," Jack explained. "The star connotes the angel who bore it. Lucifer. The Morningstar." The Fallen Angel.

Schuyler traced the outline of the triglyph with her fingertips. "Have you ever seen this before?"

"I feel like I have . . . somewhere . . . in the past. I can't remember," he said, studying it as he kept his torch focused on the symbol. "It may be a ward, to keep the spell of doom around this place."

"Somehow I don't think that's it." Schuyler couldn't take her eyes off the triglyph. The symbol had a hypnotic, lulling effect, which was only broken by the sound of footsteps. "That's Ghedi. Let's not tell him about this until we find out what he knows."

Jack nodded and pointed his torch toward the cave entrance to help guide the way. The priest was breathing heavily when he reached them. "Did you find her?" he asked, looking around nervously.

"No. We should go. If she's not here, we have to let her family know," Jack replied.

Ghedi looked relieved, and they began their upward climb.

"Wait." Schuyler stopped. She'd heard something familiar—a small silent whimpering in the distance, the sound of muted anguish from one who is suffering. "There." She ran into the deepest recess of the cave, toward a small crouched figure, bound and shackled in the dark.

"MariElena," Schuyler whispered. She crouched down and put a hand on the girl's brow. Hot. Burning. Hopefully it was a fever from exposure, and nothing else.

The girl stirred and whimpered again.

The priest crossed himself and knelt down next to her.

"Do you know where you are?" Schuyler asked in Italian.

"In the cavern," MariElena replied without opening her eyes. "Near the dried-up creek."

Jack took off his jacket and put it around the young girl's shoulders. "Do you know why you are here?" he asked.

"They brought me here," she answered dully.

"Who were they?" Schuyler asked. "What did they do to you?"

In answer, MariElena shuddered involuntarily as if having a seizure.

Schuyler held the girl in her arms and continued to

soothe her. "It's all right, it's all right," she whispered. "You're going to be okay. You're safe now."

But the girl only shook her head and shut her lips tight.

"There now," Ghedi said, placing a cool handkerchief on her feverish brow.

Schuyler prodded her with the glom, took the chance to look into the girl's memories. The boyfriend had driven her out of town and into the mountains. He had taken her straight into the forest. Then there was nothing. Mist and vapor. The girl had woken to find herself bound in the cave.

Jack cut off the bonds and helped the girl to her feet. Schuyler took her right shoulder. The girl staggered and swayed between them, then fell to a faint.

"Here, let me help," Ghedi said, rushing to MariElena's side.

Things happened too quickly after that, because the next thing Schuyler knew, the priest was holding a ivory-handled knife against the girl's throat.

"What are you doing?" Schuyler cried, reaching toward the priest and the girl, as Jack came at them from behind.

"What I am meant to do," Ghedi said, holding the girl, who was now as limp as a rag doll in his arms, the glittering blade pressed at her jugular. MariElena's thin blouse fluttered against her neck, and as it did, Schuyler caught a glimpse of the triglyph again. This time it was branded on the girl's chest. The interlocking circles. The animal. Lucifer's sigil. It glowed in the dark like a beacon.

Schuyler was focusing on sending a powerful compulsion to stop the priest when she was hit by an unexpected blow that sent her crashing against the stone walls. It did not come from Ghedi, who looked momentarily confused. It came from someone or something else.

"Schuyler!" Jack's anguished cry echoed through the cavern.

I'm okay, she wanted to send, but found she could not. She could not move, she could not speak, she was paralyzed in every sense. She struggled to find a way out of her bondage—but this spell was not as easy as Iggy's. There were traces of dark magic in it, forbidden workings that made her bindings as solid as rock.

Unlike the ragtag company of farmers searching for a missing daughter, this was an ambush by a vampire with a vampire's speed and strength.

"Come quietly or your girl will make a pretty bonfire," the vampire told Jack, holding out Venator rope and motioning for Jack to tie his wrists with it. In his other hand he held a torch burning with the Black Fire.

No! Schuyler sent, finding her voice in the twilight even though she was still completely immobilized.

Why are you doing this? Do you work for the Countess?

I don't work for anybody. I'm not in any Coven. This is all for me.

So it had come to this, Schuyler realized. Mimi had placed a bounty on Jack's life, and the vampire was out to collect.

Please! No! We have money—we can pay you. Let me pay you for his life. Please! Schuyler sent.

Sorry, missy. But I'm pretty sure you won't be able to pay as much as Mimi Force.

The bounty hunter shuffled up toward Schuyler, and she could see his feral, drawn face hovering over hers.

"I will come freely. Let her go," Jack declared in a calm, clear voice as he surrendered. The vampire tightened the knots, drawing blood from Jack's wrists. Once Jack was secured, the vampire whispered a few words over the flame, which died down until the torch resembled nothing but a gray chunk of coal. He quickly tucked it into his back pocket.

Ghedi looked uneasily at the renegade vampire, but once he understood that the vampire had no quarrel with him, his face became set as he prepared himself for the ugly task ahead.

MariElena would die.

Jack would be taken.

There was nothing Schuyler could do but scream.

THIRTEEN

Angel Time

There was so little time to do anything out in the real world, where she had been captured and attacked. So Schuyler looked inward, into her soul and into the glom. Time did not exist in the same way in the inner universe.

She opened her eyes to the murky waters of the twilight world, and felt the heavy constriction of the dark spell that held her captive. In the glom, her bindings manifested as a coil of snakes writhing around her skin. She felt their scaly wetness wrap around her body, clutching her ever more tightly. They were all around, slithering against her waist, around her legs, slipping through her fingers. She could smell their oozy stink, and shivered to hear the rasp of their tongues.

A stasis spell worked as part of the compulsion—mind control—essentially an order to make you believe you were trapped, which was why it was one of the most difficult factors to master. You had to stop believing what was right in front of you.

Schuyler focused on the snake nearest to her head. She could feel its cold reptile body working its way around her shoulders. She turned so she could face it eye to eye. It was a fearsome king cobra, its hood spread as it reared to attack. It bared its fangs and hissed.

But before it could strike, Schuyler overcame her revulsion and reached down to grip it by its tail, and with one fluid motion, she pulled the snake away from her body and crushed its serpent head under her heel.

In a flash she was back in the real world of the cave, holding her mother's sword. "Stop!" she commanded, her voice ringing with fury.

The priest hastened to thrust the knife through the girl's neck, but before the blade could penetrate her skin, Schuyler had parried it away, and it clattered on the rocks. MariElena fell to the ground, and Ghedi with her, felled by Schuyler's compulsion to surrender.

That was all Jack needed. With a vehement roar, he broke his bonds and transformed into the fearsome Angel of Destruction, magnificent black wings sprouting from his back, his horns curled to sharp diamond points, and his eyes a bloodcurdling crimson. He picked up the now quivering bounty hunter and crushed him against his talons.

"Jack, no. Don't kill him!" Schuyler cried. *Let there be no blood spilled today.*

"Listen to the girl. . . ." the bounty hunter gurgled.

Schuyler put a gentle hand on Abbadon's feathered extensions, feeling the majestic power underneath their silky weight. She had been frightened once, to see him in this light, but now that she saw his terrifying true face, she found it beautiful.

He turned to her; as Abbadon he looked at once nothing at all like Jack, and yet more like him than ever. *He was going to hurt you.*

Please, my love.

Then he was Jack again, ruddy-cheeked and handsome. He pulled the bounty hunter to his feet. "Go. Tell my sister that her parasite has failed. Tell her that nothing and no one can bring me back." That was all the bounty hunter needed to hear. He disappeared before taking another breath.

Schuyler collapsed into Jack's arms, and they held each other.

I thought I was going to lose you, she sent.

Never. We shall never be separated. Jack bent his head against her shoulder, and she leaned on his chest so that she could hear his heart beating a steady, ordered rhythm against hers.

Never.

The Artist's Studio

In the morning, Tomi returned to her work at the studio. The Master
would not return until tomorrow, and there was still so much to do.
She greeted her fellow assistants and took her place at the back of the
room, where she resumed carving a relief meant for the east doors of
the Baptistery. The work was painstaking and exact, but Tomi reveled
in it, finding glory and beauty in the fine details. She was soon lost in
thought, her hands quickly running over the marble, while her mind lin-
gered over the events of a month before.

What did it mean that a human carried the mark of the Prince of
Darkness? Had their old foe found a way back to Earth? It could not
be. They had sent the devil down to hell, had locked Caligula behind an
impenetrable gate. Together they had sent the Order of the Seven out to
the world, to secure the paths of the Dead. The man wearing the Citadel
robes had been an impostor. No one had ever seen him before. He was
a stranger to their town. Andreas believed that the human had lied and
that the creature was no demon, but Tomi was more given to anxiety

She was sixteen years old; already she knew who she was and what she was meant for in this world. After the crisis in Rome, in every consequent lifetime, the Venators had made it their mission to track down the remaining Silver Bloods who were trapped on the other side of the Gate and still walked the Earth. No one else in the Coven knew about the errant surviving Silver Bloods. It was a secret the Venators kept in order to keep peace in the community. The Blue Bloods had nothing to fear from the Croatan; Andreas had kept their people safe for hundreds of years. Hunting down the Croatan was as routine as a cat chasing field mice. Necessary and efficient.

But now this. Tomi saw the triglyph again, the blood etching on the man's arm, and dropped her knife, making an ugly smear on the bas-relief. The Master would not be pleased.

"You are troubled, my friend," Gio said, picking up the knife and handing it back to her. "Do not be. We will take care of this."

She nodded. "I only wish Dre was here." Andreas del Pollaiuolo was the youngest adviser to the court of Lorenzo de Medici, working to solidify the family's grasp on power in Florence over the other ruling families of the city. The Medicis' banking interests spanned all of Europe with a network of branches in all the major cities. It was a cover that made it easy for Dre to travel the continent without arousing suspicion.

But Tomi knew there was another reason Dre worked so hard to ensure the Medicis' influence would reach far beyond their beautiful city. The crisis in Rome was forever utmost in his mind. While he had succeeded in banishing Lucifer from the world, he had been unable to halt the decline of the glorious Republic that the Morningstar, as Caligula, had corrupted. Rome was lost.

Dre was intent on rebuilding its glory. He was determined to finish what he started, pledging to resurrect the glory of Rome and the culture of antiquity, and vaulting it to a new level. Already he had rewritten the Code of the Vampires to shape human history and imbue mankind with Blue Blood sensibility and values—the celebration of art, life, beauty and truth. He would bring about mankind's rebirth, he told her, in their numerous conversations about what they hoped to achieve in this cycle. He had already given it a name: The Renaissance.

But all this work took her beloved away from her, and since the night of the chase, they hardly had a moment together.

He was always like this, her Michael. Andreas. Cassius. Menes. Whatever his name was, he was always hers. Her strength, her love, her reason for being. They would fight this new threat together. She would await his return and then impress upon him the urgency to unmask their hidden enemies and discover the truth behind the Red Blood's mark.

PART THE SECOND

MIMI FORCE,
REGENT OF THE COVEN

New York

The Present

FOURTEEN

Vipers' Nest

*S*elf-pity was not a word in Mimi Force's vocabulary. Instead of cursing the loneliness and isolation she felt from losing both her twin and the man she loved—two separate people for the first time in her long and immortal life—she busied herself with Conclave business, burying her grief and rage in her work and finding solace in presiding over the bureaucratic administration of a large and flailing organization.

That old hag Cordelia Van Alen used to describe the current era as "the twilight of the vampires"—as if a heavy velvet curtain were falling across the stage, and it was time for the Blue Bloods to *exeunt* left. (Mimi always liked those old English words. *Exeunt* was a vastly more interesting way to shuffle off this mortal coil—as if the vampires were ready to take their bows in front of a standing ovation rather than simply limping away into the sunset.)

If this *was* their end, her end, then it was an intolerable one. Mimi hadn't lived a multitude of lifetimes to end up so alone, without the security blanket of Jack to steady her, without Kingsley's endearing arrogance to keep her on her toes. She wasn't going to give up so easily.

Mimi opened the door to her new office. A week ago, ever since Forsyth Llewellyn had gone missing after the "bonding disaster"—as everyone called the travesty that had been her bonding day—the Conclave had agitated for a new leader. To her surprise, it was her name that had come up in the draw. A week after the disastrous bonding, Ambrose Barlow, a sprightly gentleman of a hundred and one years (cycle extensions had been granted to allow Emeritus members of the Conclave to serve), and Minerva Morgan, the sharp-tongued Conclave Elder who had been one of Cordelia Van Alen's closest friends, had met her after school and pressed their case. Mimi had refused to put up her name for Regis— not while Charles was still alive somewhere—but had agreed to accept the title of Regent, the Coven's titular head in a leaderless time.

She settled into the cushy, ergonomic office chair she'd ordered, and called up the Committee database on her desktop. There was so much to do: identify the strongest Committee members and promote them to the flagging Conclave, oversee the Venator staff, induct new blood into the junior Committee—the list went on and on. Forsyth had left everything a mess—it seemed the man had had no interest in anything other than the Conclave while he had been in power, and many of the subcommittees (Health of Human Services, Transformation Centers) were grossly understaffed.

Speaking of Forsyth: no one knew where Bliss was either. The two had probably absconded together, for all Mimi knew. Good riddance. After Forsyth Llewellyn's disappearance, the Venators had found evidence that Mimi's predecessor had been harboring their deepest enemy and was instrumental in bringing the Croatan to the attack at the cathedral. Forsyth was the traitor in the Conclave, the snake in their midst.

As for Kingsley, Mimi could still see his face before it had been erased by the *subvertio*. Looking at her with so much love in his eyes. Where was he now? Was he still alive? Would she ever see him again? Sometimes when she thought about him, she would find she had been staring into space for hours, just staring at the same blinking cursor on a computer screen, while the hurt in her heart throbbed and ached. Nothing made her feel better, absolutely nothing. She had tried throwing a ridiculous amount of money at the problem, over-shopping on her credit cards, and had consulted an array of healers and therapists. But even after a month, nothing had helped. Without the many Conclave meetings and conference calls that allowed her to escape her sadness for a little while, she thought she might go insane with despair.

Of course, even though she was Regent now, she still had to finish out her senior year. More pressing business had to wait until AP exams were over, according to Trinity, who did not accept any excuses, even the governance of the community, for missing schoolwork. Her mother only allowed her a few hours a day to devote to her new position. It had been enough of a blow that Jack was wanted and missing; Trinity wouldn't let Mimi slack off on her studies as well.

If at first she had been reluctant to take the title, Mimi had slowly warmed to the idea, especially once she'd realized she could use it to her advantage. As the fearless leader of the Coven, she could do anything she wanted. It was the first week of November. She'd been in office for a month now, and had yet to wield her power over something she dearly wanted—taking care of the Coven had come first. But today was finally the day. Today she would have a little conversation with one Oliver Hazard-Perry. She'd had him fetched from the bowels of the Repository, and her secretary rang to inform her of his presence in the waiting room.

"Send him in, Doris," Mimi ordered, preparing herself for what was sure to be a fight. The wretched human Conduit was her only link to her traitorous brother, and she was determined to beat any information as to Jack's whereabouts out of him.

Oliver walked into her office. She barely knew the boy, and in the past had only paid attention to him because of his proximity to her rival for Jack's affections, but even she could discern that he looked different since she last saw him—something in his eyes—a hooded stillness that wasn't there before. But then again, who hadn't changed since the bonding disaster? She herself had looked in the mirror the other day and had been horrified to see a haggard, grief-stricken spinster looking back at her. Tragedy was wreaking havoc on her sun-kissed cover-girl looks. It had to stop.

"You rang?" Oliver asked. His face was a mask of deeply felt suffering, so it surprised her that he could still made jokes.

Mimi tossed her hair over her shoulder. "That is not the way a human addresses his superiors."

"Forgive me, madam." Oliver smirked. He made himself comfortable in the guest chair. "How may I be of service?"

She got right to the point. "You know where they are." The minute her brother had left town, Mimi had sent an army of Venators and mercenaries after him, but so far none had been successful in bringing him to justice. Once Jack had left the Coven, he had disavowed its protection as well, so that his spirit was not traceable through the glom.

"*They?*" he asked, cocking an eyebrow.

"My brother and his . . ." Mimi could not bring herself to say it. "You know where they went; the Venators told me you were there at the airport when they disappeared."

Oliver clasped his hands together and looked firm. "I can neither agree nor disagree with that statement."

"Don't be coy. You know where they are and you have

to tell me. You work for me now. You dare defy the Code? You know the punishment for Conduit insubordination is twenty years in solitary," she snarled, leaning over her desk and baring just a hint of her fangs.

"Oh, we're bringing the Code into this, are we?"

"If I have to," Mimi threatened. As a Repository scribe, Oliver was low man on the totem pole. He was collateral—nothing more than an underpaid clerk. Whereas she was Mimi Force. She was Regent now! She was the only thing keeping the Coven together at this point.

Oliver smiled a crafty smile. "Then in my defense, I must plead the Fifth Commandment."

"The Fifth?" Bells of recognition began to ring in the back of her head, but Mimi ignored them. She was all-powerful; he was the one playing games. Crush the human cockroach! No one dared defy Azrael when she wanted something.

"Forgive me if I sound patronizing, but according to the Fifth Commandment of the Code of the Vampires, there is such a thing as Vampire-Conduit Confidentiality. It is within my rights not to divulge any information about my former Blue Blood mistress. Look it up. You'll find it in the Repository Files. You can't touch me."

Mimi picked up a Tiffany lamp from her desk and hurled it at Oliver, who managed to dodge it at the last moment.

"Temper, my dear. Temper."

"Out of my office, worm!"

Oliver made a show of slowly straightening up and gathering his things. It was obvious he was enjoying her frustration. Yet before he left, he turned around to address her one last time, and his voice was gentle. "You know, Mimi, like you, I am also bereft. I'm aware it doesn't mean very much coming from me, but I am sorry this happened to you. I loved Schuyler very much, and I know how much you loved Jack."

Jack! No one had *dared* say that name to her face. And it wasn't love she felt for her twin, but a confusing whirl of shock and sorrow. Love? Whatever love she had left had turned into a bright, glittering hate, a hate she nursed deep in her soul until it shone like an emerald.

"Love," Mimi hissed. "You familiars know nothing about love. Delusional human, you never felt love; you only felt what the Kiss *required* you to feel. It's not real. It never was."

Oliver looked so wounded that for a moment Mimi wanted to take it back, especially since his were the first words of sympathy she had heard since losing everyone who had ever meant anything to her. Still, it had felt good taking her hate and directing it outward. Too bad Oliver had tried to help. Fool: he'd only stood in the line of fire.

FIFTEEN

Seen Your Video

The punching bag swayed back and forth like a pendulum, and Mimi gave it another satisfying kick—right in the center. She'd come straight to the gym after leaving her office for the day. She didn't need anyone's pity, least of all that stupid Repository scribe's. Times really had to be tough if a human was feeling sorry for a vampire. Especially one of her lineage and status. What was the world coming to? She had survived the crisis in Rome and weathered the journey to Plymouth, only to be the object of a Red Blood's sympathy? Absolutely ridiculous. She punched the bag again, sending it whirling to the other side of the room. Her muscles ached from spending the last four hours kickboxing the crap out of it.

She pictured Jack's bloody face bowed in humiliation and begging for mercy. How satisfying it would be to unleash her fury at last. Every minute of every day she was consumed by revenge; she lived and breathed it; her anger fueled her will to live. Where was he? What was he doing? Was he even thinking of her at all?

Why couldn't she just leave it alone, she wondered as the bag spun and knocked her off balance for a moment. She didn't even *want* Jack anymore—she had understood as much at the altar. He didn't want her, but she didn't want him either. So why was she so obsessed with his death? Because *someone* had to pay for Kingsley's. Kingsley was gone; he was dead, or trapped—it didn't matter. It was easier to feel a murderous rage against her brother than an overwhelming grief at her lover's demise. It killed Mimi to think that Jack had survived while Kingsley had not. That Jack was happy, somewhere out there with his half-blood concubine, and she was alone. *Someone* had to pay for the scope of what she had lost—someone had to pay. If Mimi couldn't be happy then she certainly didn't see why anyone else should be.

It was beyond tiring being angry all the time, and Mimi craved the physical exhaustion her punishing workouts brought her. Most days after leaving the gym she would go home numb and too beat to do much else other than laze on the sofa with her laptop, replying to IMs and updating her status on social networking sites. On this particular night, the town house was empty when she returned, which was not a surprise. Trinity was out at some society function, as usual. The house was too big for just the two of them. The maids kept to themselves, and the silence was so depressing that on most nights Mimi had both the stereo and the television blasting while she surfed the Web.

She threw her smelly gym clothes into the hamper and took a quick shower. Still wearing her bathrobe, she fired up her computer and clicked on her in-box, scrolling through the list of unread messages. Blinking at the top was an e-mail from an unknown address. Even though the Committee's tech team begged her to stop doing so, Mimi routinely disregarded warnings about the danger of Internet viruses hiding in unknown e-mails, and as a result her computer crashed several times a month. She couldn't help it; she was too curious to not open them.

She clicked it open. The e-mail was empty save for a link. Mimi hit it, and braced for the onslaught of computer havoc, her system breaking down, or some kind of dirty video appearing on her screen. The link did take her to a video, but not one of the pornographic variety.

The screen showed a hazy video, a bunch of jerky handheld camera angles, until finally Mimi noticed that the two dark shapes in the middle of the screen were actually teenagers necking on a couch.

So it was one of *those* videos after all, she thought, ready to close the window. But something stopped her. As the camera zoomed closer, she realized the teenagers weren't just hooking up. The girl's face was obscured by her long hair, but Mimi could see that her lips were pressed against the boy's neck, and blood was running down her chin, as his body twitched and convulsed in an ecstatic spasm.

It was all too familiar—the boy's fervid motions, the way the girl was holding him—gentle enough to keep his frenzy in check and yet firm so that she could keep him right where she wanted him. How many times had Mimi done the same exact thing in the same exact position? It was practically out of the Committee handbook. You didn't want a familiar's head to roll back lest he or she lose oxygen, or choke on his or her own tongue.

Mimi watched, frozen in her seat, as the girl pulled away, and for a moment, the camera zeroed in on her ivory fangs, and they caught the light, revealing their needle-sharp beauty—so much finer and sharper than any computer-enhanced prop. Meanwhile, the boy slumped back into the couch, drugged, defeated, and for the next forty-eight hours, useless. The girl, her face still in shadow, kissed him sweetly on the lips and stood up from the couch.

On the bottom of the screen was a date and a time stamp. That was just last weekend, Mimi thought, as the image cut to a larger room, where many more teenagers were gathered. Wait, wait, wait! There was something familiar about that room, with those damask curtains and that Renoir on the wall. If you got too close to the painting, you tripped the silent alarm and the house majordomo would shoo you away. She'd been to that apartment many times. It was Jamie Kip's parents' penthouse and this was his eighteenth birthday after-party. Mimi had been there Friday night. She'd left early, bored by the scene. The newest Committee members were little eager beavers, hopped up on their first taste of blood, and she was still too angry to have much fun.

When the camera focused on the girl again, her back was turned, and she disappeared in a blink of an eye, only to reappear across the room, laughing next to the keg. This was no trick, no visual effect, no clever editing. It was clear that the girl had been in one place and then without any natural explanation for it, in another. Dear God, don't tell me. . . . The camera caught more vampire tricks. Stupid junior members showing off—someone lifting the grand piano with one hand, another party guest turning into fog. The usual juvenile exuberance, vampires drunk on their newfound powers that came with the Transformation.

A cold knot began to form in Mimi's stomach. Who the hell was videotaping them? Blue Blood parties were strictly closed—vampires and familiars or soon-to-be-familiars only. That was the policy. This was against every rule in the Code. This was *exposure*. It was online. Had anyone else seen this? Mimi felt the hair on the back of her neck tingle.

The scene faded and words appeared. *Vampires are real. Open your eyes. They are all around us. Do not believe the lies they tell. The Mistress lives!*

The who? The what? Mimi was still trying to absorb what she'd read when the screen shifted again. Another room, but now the girl was shown tied up, bound and blindfolded, with a gag in her mouth, still unrecognizable. That was Venator rope, Mimi could tell from the silver stitching. What was going on? What the hell was happening? Who was that girl?

The screen faded to black, replaced by more text.

On the eve of the shadow crescent . . .

Watch the vampire burn.

A match was struck, and a fire burned, filling the screen. Smoky dark flames that danced around an ebony center. The Black Fire of Hell.

Mimi shut off the computer, banging down the screen on her laptop. She found she was trembling. It was a joke, wasn't it? Someone from the party had decided to make a funny video. That was all it was. It had to be. Jamie Kip and Bryce Cutting probably put it together to spook her. They still couldn't accept she was their Regent. It was just a joke to them.

Still, Mimi didn't sleep well that night. She wished she could just forget about it, delete it, and like any normal teenager, go back to counting the number of her friends online. But she couldn't. She was their leader. She was responsible for the safety of every vampire in the Coven. She wasn't going to lose one on her watch. No way. Not this time. Not after Charles's blind denial of the existence of the Silver Bloods . . . and Forsyth's betrayal of the Conclave. Whatever this was—a new Silver Blood threat, or something else?—she had to be prepared to deal with it. She had to take action. This video had been sent to her for a reason.

SIXTEEN

The Conspiracy

*T*he sixty-inch monitor on the wall showed the vampire's face full of terror, frozen on the screen. Mimi looked around the conference table on Monday morning to make sure everyone had a chance to absorb it. She had skipped class for this, but even Trinity could not argue that this was less important than passing AP Mandarin.

Around the table sat members of the Conspiracy, the subcommittee that handled human-vampire relations and disseminated false information about the vampires into the human world. Conspiracy members included several best-selling novelists, one of whom had popularized the amusing idea that instead of burning to death, vampires smelled like roses in the sun, as well as film producers who kept the slash-and-behead theory alive and well in numerous blockbuster horror movies. More than a few were annoyed to have been pulled from their lucrative jobs for an emergency meeting.

The Conspiracy had not met as a body in many years.

Seymour Corrigan, Conclave Elder and head of the Conspiracy, opened the discussion. "Any ideas where this might have come from?"

"Looks like one of your jobbers, Harry," joked Lane Barclay-Fish, the author of *Blood and Roses* and said mastermind of the floral-smelling vampires conceit. He turned to Harold Hopkins, the executive producer of a popular vampire soap opera currently running on a prestigious cable network.

"Not me—in my show the humans only use our blood as vitamins. You know, long life and all that," chortled Harold, a bald vampire who wore sunglasses indoors.

Warden Corrigan cleared his throat. "I fail to see the amusement in this enterprise."

"You guys, Seymour's right, this isn't funny," Mimi said. "This is a video from a real party. That's one of us up there, not one of Harold's overpaid actresses." It galled her that after everything that happened, they could still be so glib when one of them was missing. She knew they were just covering up their fear, but it was in poor taste.

"Right, right," Lane apologized. "I say we let the Red Bloods think it's a movie trailer. One of Josie's, maybe."

Josephine Mara was the hottest young director in the business. She had the pinched, stressed look of someone perennially on deadline. In the past year she had helmed several "underground" horror films to major success. It was easy enough to make horror films. As a vampire she didn't need to pay for special effects. She just created them. "Sure, why not?" Josephine smiled thinly. "I'll say it's a follow-up to *Eidolon Memory*," she said, naming her most recent hit, a haunted-house ghost story set in a girls' boarding school.

"Remember when one of the familiars penned a tell-all memoir in the 1800s?" Harold asked.

"Yes, thank God we got her publisher to categorize it as a novel," Lane said, nodding. "What was that woman thinking? And that title! *Longing for Love Forever*, jeez. Lord Byron has a lot to answer for."

"He did have quite the taste for the ladies. Bite 'em and leave 'em. Meanwhile, the poor lady is stuck with the yearning and all that. Must be difficult. A pity." Harold shrugged.

"I miss the old days, when it was so easy," Lane sighed. "Remember when we came up with Count Dracula? That was fun. Sent scores of tourists to Romania! Red Bloods will believe anything."

"That was a good prank," agreed Annabeth Mahoney, who had created a popular video game called "Blood Wars," which pitted vampires against each other. In Mimi's opinion, sometimes the Conspiracy played too fast and loose with disseminating untruths that were a little too close to the real thing.

"Gentlemen, ladies," Mimi interrupted, clearing her throat. "As much as I'm enjoying this trip down memory lane—or rather, manipulated memory lane—this is not just a security breach. Even if we're able to convince the Red Bloods this is yet another Hollywood fiction, it shows that whoever put this together knows too much about us, which puts us all in danger. That's hellfire up there. And one of our own is missing." Mimi turned to the twin Venators seated to her right. She'd pulled Sam and Ted Lennox from their previous assignment to work on this one. "Sam, what do we know so far?"

Sam took the mouse and clicked on an icon on the screen, minimizing the video and pulling up a photograph of a pretty, red-haired girl. It was the same girl from the video. "The Blue Blood in question is Victoria Taylor. Seventeen. Duchesne senior. She was last seen at a party thrown by Jamie Kip at his apartment, where this video was shot. Nothing irregular in her Transformation as far as the Committee can tell. Blue veins at fifteen, the hunger, all that. No deviant behaviors, no aberrant actions in her history. We checked the Rep Files. Family is solid Coven stock."

He clicked on the mouse again to show another photograph. This one was of a good-looking boy with messy blond hair and dimples. "This is her human familiar, Evan Howe, sixteen, Duchesne junior, also missing since the night of the party. Ted, you want to take it from here?" he asked his brother.

"Sure." Ted pulled a reporter's notebook from his coat pocket and began to read from it. "So far, the video has been circulating on the Internet, and to Lane's suggestion, it's already happened. The Red Bloods think it's a movie trailer."

The members nodded.

"So we've been puffing up that idea by spreading rumors that a movie called *Suck* is coming out. It's a documentary, handheld, horror type of thing. So far, the public seems to be buying it. Apologies in advance to the more talented members of the group—I wouldn't presume to know how to do your job. Sam and I had one of the tech people jazz up this footage, and this new trailer is making the rounds on the Web now, too."

Sam clicked on the mouse and the horrifying video played again. At the end, it displayed a tagline. "*Suck*," it read in bloodred letters. "Coming to theaters near you."

"I'll get it up on my IMDB profile as soon as possible," Josephine agreed. "*Suck* . . . I like it. Good title."

"So that covers the security risk, at least," Sam sighed. "But on to the real issue. We believe this is a genuine threat and that Victoria has been taken by hostiles. We haven't gotten a bead yet on where she is or who's holding her. Her parents are in Mustique for the season. They're flying back today, but they haven't seen her in months, and as far as I could gather, they don't seem to know very much about her day-to-day life."

Typical Blue Blood parents, Mimi thought. Since their "children" weren't their children at all, most vampires had very loose family connections. Mimi was always grateful that

Charles and Trinity, no matter that they were only her cycle parents, had been more attentive than indifferent. It could have been much worse, as the Taylors showed.

"And the Red Blood?" she asked.

"His parents were a little more on the ball. They filed a missing persons report last week. The school is keeping it hush-hush and out of the papers, of course. No one wants any more bad publicity. But if he doesn't turn up soon, those Red Bloods are going to FNN." Sam smiled an ironic smile. "Usually the Force News Network thrives on this kind of stuff. Missing rich kids. Scandal on the Upper East Side, etcetera. But I take it they'll sit on this one?" he asked Mimi.

"Of course. They'll get nothing from us," Mimi promised.

"We traced the IP address of the computer that posted the video. It went to a ghost. We're having tech untangle that one," Sam continued. "The shadow crescent is the first sign of the waning moon. About seven days away. We're treating this as a countdown situation. This is Day One. Which means we've only got six days left."

"And you're sure this isn't the Silver Bloods?" Mimi asked.

"It's not like them to go public with this kind of stuff. They're not . . . modern, shall we say," Sam answered. "No. We're quite sure this is something else. We think it might be a human threat."

Annabeth gasped. "Are humans even capable of something like this? That's insane. It's like the sheep ambushing the shepherd."

"Unfortunately, it's not impossible," Ted said. "It's a numbers issue, and there have always been more of them than there are of us."

"If they find out who we are," Sam said, "who knows what could happen. The Conclave has always made certain that our existence remain invisible to their world. Because if not—"

"It can't happen, regardless," Ted said, interrupting his brother's thought. "We're going to shut this down."

"From what we can tell, the person who made this video is a human who's close to our community," Sam said gravely. "A familiar is unlikely, since the *Caerimonia* seals the human's loyalty to his or her vampire partner; a human familiar is rendered incapable of doing harm. So it's got to be someone else. A human who knows everything about us and yet is not bound to a vampire. We've checked the records to see what humans, if any, have access to the Kip residence, and the Conduits are our best guess. It's a stretch, but they are given keys to the Repository, which means they could possibly have access to hellfire."

Hellfire was kept under the Conclave's highest security in the deepest basement of the Repository. It was almost impossible to think that a lowly Conduit would be able to break in without alerting the Venator guard, but there was no other explanation right then.

Mimi sucked in her cheeks. "You will interrogate all the Conduits. Torture them if you have to. Do not spare them any mercy."

"That's the thing we want to talk to you about. We're planning to scan their memories, of course. But someone who's made something like this knows how we work and is likely to have planned ahead and may have protected themselves. As Conduits, they are taught a little knowledge of the glom, and a little knowledge goes a long way."

"How about if one of their own interviews them, trips them up somehow?" Mimi suggested, thinking immediately of Oliver. "I have just the person to ask." She had read the glowing reports from the Repository. He had a high reputation for loyalty and discretion. Plus, if he reported directly to her, she could keep a closer eye on him and monitor his communications. But getting him to agree to help was another matter. If only she hadn't been so rude to him the other day. This was going to be tricky, she could already tell.

"Could work, why not?" Sam Lennox agreed.

Lane rapped on the table. "That sounds like a plan. Are we done here? I'm meeting my editor for lunch at Michael's and I'm late. We're talking sequel."

"More roses?" Annabeth teased.

"A veritable rose parade of the undead, my friends." Lane raised his fist in a show of solidarity. "The Conspiracy lives!"

Warden Corrigan coughed into his handkerchief.

"Looks like the Venators have it covered. On our end, we'll make sure the Web is all over this movie. We'll squash any suggestion it might be 'real.' Although it might make for good publicity," Harold said, looking meaningfully at Josephine, who nodded.

"Good point," Mimi said. "Josephine, you'll start production on that movie. Lane, Harold, Annabeth, continue doing what you've been doing. Thank you for taking the time to meet with us." Mimi bid Conspiracy members good-bye as they filed out of the room, shaking Seymour Corrigan's hand as he left.

"Too many members of the Conspiracy think their jobs are nothing but propaganda and artifice. This abduction is serious business," the Warden said.

Mimi nodded. "We'll find whoever's behind this. You have my word."

"And us? What about the other assignment?" Ted asked, gathering his papers.

"You mean my brother?" Mimi asked as Warden Corrigan shuffled out.

Sam nodded. "We have word that he is no longer under the protection of the Countess. We were about to start a more exhaustive search."

Mimi sighed. She wanted more than anything to set the Venator twins loose on Jack and Schuyler. Bring that traitor brother of hers to heel. Talk about burning. But she knew it would have to wait. She couldn't turn her back on poor Victoria Taylor.

"No. Focus on this for now. We need to find this girl. And whoever made this video."

Ted saluted her. "Whatever you say, ma'am."

The team disbanded, and Mimi lingered at the table, drumming her fingers. She felt a rush of the old excitement running through her veins. She was suddenly not paralyzed by hate, or stifled by an inchoate frustration; she was filled with purpose. She was going to find whoever did this and crush them under the point of her spiked heels. And she would enjoy it. No one threatened the vampires. No one.

SEVENTEEN

Recruit

s Mimi predicted, Oliver ignored her request to meet, so she had to track him down the following afternoon. He was still a student at Duchesne so it wasn't that hard. She found him standing in front of his locker, putting away his trumpet after practice. Duchesne didn't have anything as common as a marching band, but it did have a student orchestra that performed at the Kennedy Center every year.

"I didn't know you played," she said.

"You don't know a lot of things about me," Oliver grumbled. "What do you want, Force? Got another lamp to break?"

Mimi crossed her arms in front of her chest and frowned. "Why didn't you come to my office yesterday afternoon like my secretary asked you to?"

He shrugged and picked up his book bag. "I figured you

wanted the same thing, and the answer's still no."

His disrespect annoyed her, and although she knew it wouldn't help to antagonize him any further, she couldn't resist. "Why do you still keep a picture of her in your locker? It's pathetic, you know. It's not like she cares about you. Not anymore. If she ever did."

Oliver sighed noisily. He rolled his eyes to the heavens. "Please stop talking."

"Like I said yesterday, you should know better than to think a vampire would ever truly care for their familiar. I mean, of course her mother's actions appear to suggest otherwise, but never in the history of the Coven has that ever happened before, and believe me—"

"Shut up, Force. You have no idea what you're talking about. And anyway, is that why you're here? To needle me about Schuyler? Don't you have anything better to do, like save the world from lunatic Silver-Blooded vampires?" He shut his locker and started to walk down the hallway, and Mimi had to run to keep up with him. The two of them garnered a few curious looks from the other students. Everyone knew they couldn't stand each other.

Mimi blocked his way and whispered in order to dissuade any potential eavesdroppers. "Look, you must have heard that the Conspiracy met yesterday."

"Yeah. I saw the trailer on the Internet. Looks like Josephine Mara's up to her tricks again. Some new movie, sure to 'suck,'" he said, using air quotes to make his point.

"That's what we want everyone else to think. The video's real."

Oliver stopped and stared at her. "Wait a minute. What do you mean it's real? As in . . ."

"As in the Coven has had its first real security breach in a hundred years. That's Victoria Taylor in the video. It was taped at Jamie Kip's apartment; he had a little get-together to celebrate his eighteenth. She's been missing since the night of the party. We have five days to find her before they burn her alive."

"But what do you need me for?" Oliver asked. "Don't the Venators have this in the bag?"

"Whoever did this knows how we operate. So we have to do something else. We need you to talk to the other Conduits—find out who might have squealed, who was at the party, who holds a grudge against us."

Oliver shook his head and raised an eyebrow. "But why should I help you?"

"You're a Repository scribe. You work for me."

"Not quite true," he said, maneuvering around Mimi. It was November in New York, and the air was chilly. Oliver huddled in his thin wool jacket. "I work for the Repository, which is under Renfield's jurisdiction. You're going to need to get a transfer from him to let me work for the Regent's office. I guarantee you it's going to take three months to get one. Renfield is very strict about policy and procedure. He doesn't like you vampires pushing him around."

Mimi gritted her teeth. Oliver was right. That old human coot wouldn't just assign her Oliver—he would make a lot of bureaucratic red tape.

"Okay, then! You should help me because there's someone in trouble and I know you're a good guy, and you're not about to let a vampire die."

"Vampires don't die," Oliver pointed out. "They get recycled to suck for another day. Pun definitely intended. Or don't you know your own history?"

"Whoever this is has the Black Fire; it will burn the blood," Mimi stressed. "Doesn't that mean anything to you?"

"Why should I care?" Oliver snapped. "It's not my problem. I'm sorry, but the answer is no. Send the transfer request to Renfield. I'll see you in three months."

Mimi was a little taken aback. Clearly the Repository had overestimated the depth of his loyalty to the Coven. She couldn't understand why he was being so antagonistic. Was it simply annoyance, a personal dislike for her, or lingering resentment over being left behind by Schuyler? Whatever it was, Mimi realized she did not care. He was being needlessly stubborn. This wasn't about the two of them, or whatever personal animosity they shared. An immortal life was on the line.

"Good God, Perry! Do you even know what you're saying?" Mimi cried. Her outburst caused several people in the courtyard to turn in their direction. Mimi glared at them. She wanted to stamp her feet, but she held her emotions in check. She was strong enough to lead an army of angels into battle, but she couldn't get one foolish Red Blood to see things her way? She decided to try something completely alien to her. "Look, I know what's going on, I know . . . that just like me, you're hurting." There. She'd admitted it.

Oliver continued to sulk, but Mimi pressed on. "I just think that—well, that maybe working on this will stop the pain for a bit. Give you something else to think about." She ran her hands through her hair in exasperation. "It's helping me, so maybe it'll help you. Even just a little."

Oliver fingered his jacket and sighed. "Well, it would help if you would ask once in a while. Instead of just demanding like you usually do."

"What do you mean?" Mimi asked, her eyes narrowed.

"I mean, you could ask nicely. You know, instead of threatening and throwing your weight around like some kind of Third World dictator. All you need is the little red cap and the epaulets and the aviators," he said, waving his hand over her. "You come across like a blond Idi Amin."

"Who's he? Never mind. You mean, like, 'Please, Oliver, will you help me find the traitor?'"

"Exactly."

Now it was Mimi's turn to roll her eyes. "Very well. Please, Oliver, will you help me find the traitor?" She felt like a three-year-old scolded by her parents for her lack of manners.

Oliver smiled. "Was it that hard, Mimi? Don't answer. I know it was. But of course I'd be glad to help, since you asked. What else do I have to do?"

EIGHTEEN

The Usual Suspects

*A*s a rule, Mimi did not enjoy the company of Red Blood boys unless they were tasty. She'd had her fill of quite a few familiars to get through the stressful week. But unless she was chomping on someone's neck and consuming their blood, she had absolutely no interest in them. So it surprised her to find she did not detest Oliver as much as she thought she would, and that working with him wasn't the torture she had expected it to be. They had four days left before the crescent moon appeared, and Mimi was relieved to find that, as she had heard, Oliver was a thorough and apt investigator. By the next morning, he had already rounded up the Conduits who had been at Jamie Kip's party.

Since only a handful of Blue Blood families still kept to the practice, there were only four Conduits in the city who could have attended the party without arousing suspicion from the other guests and pulled off the stunt. Oliver brought each suspect into a small room in the Repository that the Venators used for questioning, while Mimi watched from the other side of the double-sided glass.

Gemma Anderson took a seat across from Oliver. She was Christopher Anderson's grandniece and Conduit to Stella Van Rensslaer. "What's all this about?" she asked Oliver. "Stella said you wanted to see me as soon as possible. Have I done anything wrong? Is this about her and Corey? I told her she was draining him dry at the rate she was using. But Stella's a vamp tramp; she'll never learn."

Mimi was shocked at the flippant attitude Gemma displayed toward her betters. Is this what the Conduits said behind their backs? That the Blue Bloods were just a bunch of bloodsuckers? How rude!

"No, this has nothing to do with Corey," Oliver said. "Although if Stella is found in violation of the Forty-Eight-Hour Rest Period, the Committee will issue a reprimand. They're not enforcing it currently, as they've got bigger things to worry about right now other than Familiar Care issues. This is about Conspiracy business." He pulled up the video on his laptop and showed it to her.

"Yeah, I've seen it, so what? Some doofus vampire decided to show off on the Internet. It was bound to happen once YouTube was invented. Props for the cover-up; everyone I know wants to see *Suck*. Watch the vampire burn, good one. That'll scare the kiddies." Gemma crossed her legs and twitched her ankles impatiently.

Oliver shrugged as if to say it didn't matter either way. "I understand you were at Jamie's the night this was filmed?"

That got Gemma's attention. "That's from Jamie's party?" She looked at the screen again. "Oh my God, it is. Yeah, we were there."

"Did you notice anything unusual?" Oliver asked. "Anyone with a video camera? They're tiny these days."

She furrowed her brow and shook her head. "Not really. It all seemed like the usual bloodfest. Vampire shenanigans. Thrills and spills."

"When was the last time you saw Victoria that night?"

Gemma paused. "I think I saw her go into the back room with Evan. You know, to have their privacy. And after that, I saw her hanging out with Bryce and Froggy at the keg. Stella and I had to leave to go to another party—she wanted to meet Corey at some Riverhead shindig downtown. Wait, did something happen to Vix? I haven't seen her in school this week."

Oliver hesitated. "There was an incident yes. She came home at five in the morning blood-drunk. Her parents decided they weren't happy with the company she was keeping at Duchesne and transferred her to Le Rosey, where her mother is an alum." That was the story the Conclave was spinning, and from her vantage point behind the glass, Mimi hoped Victoria's friends would buy it.

"Really? They freaked that much? Her parents always seemed pretty cool."

"This isn't about Victoria," Oliver said. "The Conclave is

concerned about the video leak. While it is fortunate that the Conspiracy was able to deal with the matter before any Red Bloods could get suspicious, they mean to discover who was behind it. You understand exposure is a very serious concern."

Gemma nodded impatiently. "Of course."

"Can I ask how you would describe your relationship to Stella?" he asked, with a raised pen.

The pretty Conduit leaned back in her chair and crossed her arms. "I see now. The vampires think we did it. One of the human Conduits, am I right? That's why you wanted to see me."

"I didn't say that."

"No, but I'm here and I don't see anyone asking Booze or Jamie or any of those guys a bunch of questions. Their blood is Blue so they're above suspicion, while we're just the honored servants entrusted with the Big Secret, I get it." Gemma sighed. "All right, fine. I'll tell you about my relationship with Stella. Other than the fact that she borrows too many of my clothes, we're good friends. I mean—you know what I mean. Love her, hate her, it's kind of the same thing."

"You don't . . . resent her position over you?"

Gemma huffed. "No, why would I? Stella's a spoiled little vampire princess, but she's *my* spoiled little vampire princess, you know? My family has worked for the Van Rensslaers for years. Stella's like my sister—we understand each other. Don't make me get emotional, but being a Conduit—it's an honor, you know? Why would I ever do something like that?

Make a video? Put it up on the Internet? It's just . . . No."
She blinked back a few tears. "Honestly? I think we keep
the vampires' secrets better than they keep them themselves.
Bryce and those guys are always showing off when they think
no one is watching. Running too fast. Picking up a desk with
one finger. I'm surprised it hasn't happened earlier. Without
those memory wipes they use like tissues, the whole world
would know already."

The next three interviews were the same. The Conduits all
professed the same shock, the same resentment at the insinu-
ation that they would ever be capable of exposing the secrets
of the vampires, the same annoyance at the very idea. Mimi
didn't need to read their minds or taste their blood to know
they were telling the truth. She was moved by the fierce
loyalty the Conduits displayed. Why had Charles stopped
using them? She wished she knew. Mimi walked into the
room after the last Conduit left. She took a seat across from
Oliver. "So, what's the verdict? Who's our Judas?"

"Well, it's not a Conduit, at least we can rule that out.
Whoever took Victoria and made the video, it isn't one of
them." Oliver said, standing up from his chair and stretching
his arms over his head. "Alibis are all airtight. Tech has
found nothing on their computers, and the Venator scans
came in clean."

"I know, I saw the reports too," Mimi sighed. "They're
all so freaking loyal."

"What if we're going about this the wrong way?" Oliver said.

"How so?" Mimi raised an eyebrow.

"Victoria's been taken captive, and her familiar is missing too. The Venators think Evan isn't capable, but what if . . ." Oliver returned to his seat. "He was her first human familiar, and they hadn't been together long. From what I can gather, the Sacred Kiss on the couch was their first hookup."

"Are you saying Evan Howe should be a suspect?"

"In the absence of one, I'd say he's as good as any," Oliver said.

Mimi's waved her hand dismissively. "You can't seriously believe that. . . ."

"I'm just putting it out there." Oliver shrugged.

"But you of all people know how human familiars are bound to love their vampire masters by the *Caerimonia*. No familiar would ever . . . *could* ever . . ." She shook her head vehemently. "It would never happen. Even the Venators ruled it out. The Sacred Kiss precludes any of that; it's impossible."

"Nothing's impossible. Sure, it's never happened before, but it doesn't mean it *couldn't* happen in the future. Who knows? The power of the *Caerimonia* may have been corrupted somehow, or lessened, we don't know."

"But it's preposterous! They'll laugh me out of the Conclave for even suggesting it!"

Oliver was stubborn. "Even so, we've got to follow it up."

NINETEEN

Venators' Quarters

*I*t was painful to see the Lennox twins sometimes. It reminded Mimi too much of her assignment with Kingsley. She had traveled the world as part of his team for a year, keeping him at arm's length all that time except for that one hookup in Rio. Their time together in New York was too little, too late. She'd realized her true feelings for him only at the very end, and now he was gone. A bubble of grief welled up inside her, but she pushed it away—she had no time to feel sorry for herself.

She was glad Sam and Ted never brought it up—the brothers were too discreet for that. They had asked her to meet them at Venator headquarters, a former tenement building in the far West Village. It was Thursday, three days until the crescent moon, and she was getting nervous. The Venators were doing their best, but so far had turned up nothing of any significance. They should at least have a suspect, by now—a clue, something. They were Blue Bloods—keepers of the secret history, vampires who knew the truth about the world—they were not used to being threatened, to being kept in the dark.

Mimi let herself in the gate and pricked her finger on the blood-lock on the front door. The shabby interiors were the complete antithesis of the slick, polished perfection of the Force Tower. She pursed her lips at the sight of the dusty banister, the broken stairs, and the peeling wallpaper. The Venators had moved to this location in the nineteenth century, and it still looked exactly as it had back then. She had a memory-flash of visiting during debutante season, when everyone in the Coven had been called in for questioning during Maggie Stanford's disappearance.

"Up here!" A cheerful voice called. Ted stood at the top landing and waved. "Elevator's broken."

"Of course," Mimi muttered.

Dormitories occupied the first and second floors. Since the Venators traveled so much, the Committee provided housing. Many of the rooms were empty. To serve as a Venator, one had to display an extraordinary amount of courage, honor, and loyalty to the Coven in at least fifty lifetimes. But even if the Conclave had lowered the threshold for acceptance so that more vampires could join, its ranks were still stretched too thin.

Only very few Blue Bloods aspired to become Venators these days. It was as Cordelia Van Alen had said—most of the vampires were content to live their lives as little more than extra-privileged Red Bloods: humans with a touch of immortality, a little more money, and not a whole lot of responsibility. Why couldn't she get Cordelia out of her head, Mimi wondered. How could it be possible that Cordelia Van Alen, a fearmonger and conspiracy theorist who had been demoted from the Conclave, could have been so prescient, while her father, Charles Force, who had led the vampires since the beginning, had been so obtuse?

Ted ushered her into the office he shared with his brother, a cramped space stacked with books and antediluvian police technology that the brothers had collected over the years: fingerprint ink pads, analog lie detector machines, yellowing evidence tags, broken binoculars. Ted in particular had an affinity for the Red Bloods' quaint idea of law enforcement. Venators had no need for such things, as most of their work was done in the shadow world of the glom.

Still, they kept to some of the same protocol as their human counterparts. Taped to the wall were photographs of each person who had been at Jamie Kip's party that night, arranged according blood status and position: BB, RB, FAM, CON. Mimi peered at the pictures. There was her own 8x12 modeling shot right in the middle. Did that mean she herself was a suspect? she wondered. She'd hardly known Victoria even though they were in the same elite clique of friends.

"So what's up?" she asked, leaning on the messy desk

stacked with file folders waist-high. She picked up a pair of steel handcuffs and began to play with them.

Sam wheeled his chair around to face her. There were dark circles under his eyes. Mimi remembered that, of the two brothers, Sam was the one who felt the assignments more keenly, and clearly the frustration was beginning to take a toll.

"Tech has been able to zero in on the computer that uploaded the file," he said. "We traced it through the ghost connection—it zapped it from here to Moscow—and the line led us to an Internet café in the East Village. We got a list of everyone who was there the afternoon the video was sent, and each one checks out. Normal Red Blood kids, no association with the Coven." He sighed. "But the good news is we've been able to reach Victoria through the glom, so we have confirmation she's alive. Scared and mute, but alive. Here's the thing, though: her signature is being clouded—we can't get a physical location on it."

"A masking spell, maybe?" Mimi ventured.

"We've tried all the counter spells to an *oris*, but if it is a masking spell it's one we've never seen before," Ted said, looking wary, slouched against the doorway. "If it is a masking spell, whoever did this isn't going to take chances with moving her around. You've got to take off the mask to move a body. Our guess is she's still in the same room where the video was filmed, so if we can figure where that is, we can find her. We've run the video dozens of times to see if we can find anything in it that'll help us zero in on her location."

"Anything?"

Ted shook his head and tossed a crumpled piece of paper into a nearby trash can. "Not yet. But we did catch something interesting. Remember all that hoopla about subliminal messages back in the fifties? No? You weren't in cycle then? But you've heard about it, right? What we found is sort of like that, except no one is selling Coke or popcorn in this one. Show her, Sam. It's right in the beginning."

Sam fired it up on his desktop screen, and the three of them crowded around the computer to watch. He played the video on super-slow motion, one three-hundredth of a frame per second. Mimi watched as the black darkness filled the screen, and then, in a blink, there was an image of a lion mounting its mate.

Okaay . . .

"There's more," Sam said, hitting fast-forward. The next image appeared in the middle of the party shot. It showed a ram's head on a stake, dead eyes open and unblinking, tongue lolling, flies circling the carcass. The final image appeared a second before the video ended: a king cobra, coiled and ready to strike.

"So?" asked Mimi impatiently, shaking the handcuffs so they made a loud clicking sound as she pulled them apart. They were looking for a missing girl and her strike team was showing her photos from *National Geographic*.

"We think it's some sort of code, a message of some kind.

We're having Renfield take a look. See if the Repository can cough up an explanation," Ted replied.

"All right. Not sure how that helps us find Victoria, but what could it hurt." Mimi pushed off the desk and faced the boys. She would always think of them as boys, since technically, as Azrael, one of the First Born, she was centuries older, even if they were Enmortals and senior Venators to boot. "Anything else?"

"Yep," Sam said, straightening in his chair and springing forward. "We found Evan Howe. Or at least, we know where he is."

Mimi put down the handcuffs. "Does he know where Victoria could be?"

"Doubtful. But since you wanted us to check on him— we did. Figured he'd show up sooner or later, after recovering from the *Caerimonia*. You know first bite's always the hardest." Sam winced.

"And?"

Ted removed a business card from his pocket. "Witness saw him take a cab out to Newark."

"Newark? What would he be doing there?" Mimi scoffed. What would a pampered prince from the Upper East Side be doing out in some crime-ridden New Jersey township? "There's nothing for someone like Evan in Newark!"

"Nothing but abandoned buildings and a blood house." Ted handed the card to Mimi.

"No way." Mimi shuddered, reading the card. *The*

Familiars' Club, it read, in fancy red lettering.

"It's the only logical place he could be. I'm sorry," Sam said.

"I didn't know him. I'm not . . . It's just . . ." Mimi sputtered. A blood house? Evan Howe? That nice-looking boy with the dimples? He was sixteen years old . . . He was so young. . . .

"You wanted to know." Ted shrugged. "So that's where he is. But take it from us, you don't want to go there. Not worth it. This human kid's got nothing to do with whoever took Victoria. Familiars aren't made that way, you know that. And if you go out there you won't find anything but the same old story. Old as Rome."

TWENTY

The Blood House

*N*ewark was across the river just a quick shot through the tunnel and lately enjoying something of a revitalized image, but as a rule, Mimi, like many Manhattanites, avoided going to New Jersey unless it was to the airport (and thus on the way to somewhere else). Even then, she only went to Teterboro. She had left the Venator station a few hours earlier and made no comment as the car drove past the charming waterfront neighborhoods and took them deeper and deeper into a gritty industrial section. She was just glad she wasn't alone that evening.

"Right here," Oliver told his driver. "You can drop us off in front." He had been silent during the forty-minute trip, and had not appeared too surprised when she told him where they were going to look for Evan.

After she'd left the Venators, Mimi had picked him up at the Repository, where he had been since yesterday afternoon, reviewing the video over and over again, searching for clues. She told him about the three images the brothers had found.

"The scribes will figure it out. Everything's in the Repository," Oliver assured her.

"I wish I had your confidence," she said. She also hoped visiting the blood house wouldn't be a waste of time, even though the Venators certainly thought so.

Mimi followed Oliver out of the car and looked around balefully. It was a neighborhood of abandoned warehouses and empty lots. The street was littered with broken bottles and used needles. There was a junkyard lined with barbed wire, and several aimless junkyard dogs, lean and mangy, prowled the street. She shuddered.

"Come on, I think it's over here," Oliver said, leading the way to the nearest building, where Mimi saw a steel door marked with a slash of red paint.

The door opened a crack. "Members only," a raspy voice growled.

Oliver nodded to Mimi, who said her line. "I'm a friend of the club. We need a room."

The door slammed then opened again. A tough-looking middle-aged woman chewing gum blocked their entrance. Mimi had heard of lowlife vampires—they usually lived off-Coven—but she had never met one before. "You'll have to pay the nightly rate, and if you want anything else off the menu, you'll have to keep an open tab."

Mimi handed over her credit card, and she and Oliver

were allowed inside. They found themselves in a small lobby area, two armchairs sitting in a pool of red light. The house mistress looked them over. "Boy or girl?"

Mimi shrugged, unsure of what was being asked of them, so Oliver took the lead. "Er, girl, please."

They watched in morbid fascination as a group of Red Blood girls, their necks sporting fresh bites, blood dripping from their wounds, lined up in front of them. The girls looked dazed and drugged, used and drained. They wore low-cut dresses or flimsy nightgowns. Some of them were barely out of their teens.

Mimi knew all about blood houses, of course—she wasn't born yesterday, duh. They were places that familiars who had been abandoned went to experience the Sacred Kiss with any vampire. It was a disgusting practice, the *Caerimonia* was intimate and sacred, not to be squandered cheaply. While the Sacred Kiss ensured that no other vampire could take a human that had already been marked, there was an ancient, dark magic that removed the poison. It was a dangerous process that weakened the human, but those who made it to the establishment didn't much care. It was the only place left for former familiars, as well as for Blue Bloods who didn't care about using humans in this way. Needless to say, it was completely against the Code, and highly illegal. The Venators made a practice of raiding them once in a while, but it was a low priority, what with everything else going on.

It smelled like blood and misery, like love squandered

and spent. The faces of the familiars were hollow and empty, their eyes dead and glassy.

"You'll do," Mimi said, feeling sick in her stomach as she picked one of the youngest girls in the bunch.

"Second room to the right," the madam barked, pointing them to the banister.

They walked down the hallway. The rooms were barely rooms—mostly walls with curtains that shielded the couples inside. They found their assigned space and parked the girl on the bed, which was a mattress on the floor. "You'd think they'd at least spring for a futon from Ikea." Mimi curled her lip.

"Just stay here," Oliver told the girl, helping her lie down. "Sleep." He turned to Mimi. "They don't let them rest here."

Mimi nodded. She pointed down the opposite hallway. "You take those rooms, I'll do these."

"Right."

"Be careful," she told him.

"There's nothing to fear here; everyone's so gone, they won't even notice us," Oliver said grimly.

"You've been here before?" Mimi asked.

Oliver didn't answer. "Call me if you find him."

Mimi pulled back the first curtain to find a vampire feeding on two humans at once, the three of them splayed out on the bed in a languid embrace. The vampire, a blond male, looked up from the pale white throat of the nearest human girl. "Join me?" he smiled. "She's lovely."

Mimi frowned and shut the curtain. In the next stall she found a Blue Blood girl lying asleep, curled up next to a human boy. He wasn't Evan, so she left them alone. She was about to open the next curtain—Let's find out what's behind door number three! she thought somewhat hysterically—when she heard Oliver's fierce whisper carry over the sound of moaning and slurping. "He's here."

She ran to the far end of the other hallway. The curtain had been pulled back and Oliver was standing over the limp form of Evan Howe. The boy had been missing less than a week and already he was unrecognizable. Skeletal, with dirty hair, sunken cheeks, and no more dimples. No more Evan, really, Mimi thought. Not with those dead, unfocused eyes. Too many vampires sucking on a human's blood could result in a milder form of the schizophrenia that afflicted the Corrupted. Mimi remembered the dead gaze of the ram's head, and felt cold.

"He's alive," Oliver said. "Evan, get up."

The boy heaved himself to a sitting position. He leered at Mimi. "Well hello, gorgeous."

"Mimi Force." Mimi shook his hand. "Evan, we want to ask you a few questions about Victoria."

"Who?" He drooled.

"Victoria Taylor? Your . . . girlfriend?" Mimi prodded.

"Oh yeah. Vix. Haven't seen her. She left me." His eyes came alive, alert at the sound of her name.

"When was the last time you saw her?" Oliver asked gently, kneeling down to speak to the boy.

Evan slumped. "Dunno."

"You don't remember Jamie Kip's party? Last weekend?" asked Mimi.

"Who's Jamie Kip? Look, you going to suck me or what?" Evan demanded, annoyed, and began to paw at Mimi's short dress. Mimi rebuffed his efforts and exchanged a strained look with Oliver, who helped her get Evan to lie back down on the mattress, where he promptly fell asleep.

"How many vampires have had him?" Mimi whispered to Oliver.

He crossed his arms and shook his head. "I would guess a lot. . . . He's pretty messed up. I'm surprised he even remembered Victoria."

"You always remember your first," Mimi said. It was true of the familiars, at least. They never forgot—they didn't have a choice. But for the Blue Bloods? Did she remember the first human boy she'd performed the *Caerimonia* with? What was his name—Scott something? She shook her head.

"Scan him," Oliver suggested.

Mimi nodded. She prodded Evan's unconscious in the glom. She saw him wake up on Saturday morning on the couch of Jamie Kip's penthouse, alone, groggy and disoriented, but happy. Over the weekend he was still in a daze. Then it wore off. She'd seen that look before: the first flush of love. He dialed his cell phone. He was calling Victoria.

He needed her. He loved her more than ever. He went to her apartment, but she wasn't there. Called all her friends. No one knew where she was. A day went by. He started to itch. To shake. The yearning. The *Caerimonia* had bonded him to her for life. He wanted it again, for her to suck his blood, but she was gone. Now it was Tuesday. He was feverish. He was losing it. Wednesday. He didn't go home, he didn't go to school. As if in a dream, he found himself at the blood house. He'd been there since. The Venators were right: he had nothing at all to do with Victoria's disappearance. He was just another victim. Collateral damage.

"Evan, we want to take you home. Your parents are worried about you," she said, shaking him awake.

"I'm not leaving. I'm not leaving here." He shook his head. His eyes were clear again for a moment. "This is home now."

Mimi followed Oliver down the stairs. She got her credit card back, and they went out the door. She found she was shivering. How many familiars had she had? Too many to count. Had some of them ended up here when she was finished with them? Had she consigned many to this fate? Had she done this to people? To boys she had used? She hadn't loved them, but she hadn't wanted them to end up like this either. She knew she was careless and selfish—but she wasn't—she didn't—

"No," Oliver said. "I know what you're thinking, but

it's not like that. Sure, some of us succumb to it, but not all of us. You can fight it. It's called self-control. Only the weak ones end up here. Or the unlucky. Evan's vampire disappeared after first blood. That's when the yearning is the strongest. Once you do it a couple of times, you're used to it. To the feeling of being incomplete."

"So—some familiars, they're okay? Even after they never have it again?" she asked hopefully.

"Sure. Not everyone becomes addicted. It becomes this thing you learn to live with, like a sadness that doesn't go away." Oliver shrugged. "At least that's what I've heard."

They stood outside on the dirty sidewalk. Mimi felt like putting a comforting hand on Oliver's shoulder, but she didn't know if he would appreciate the gesture. Instead, she said, "You're never going to end up like him. Don't even worry about that."

"I hope not," Oliver said. "But never say never."

For a moment, Mimi hated Schuyler Van Alen more than ever, but this time it had nothing to do with Jack.

The Changeling

Florence, 1452

Giovanni Rustici, or Gio, as everyone called him, was the group's newest Venator, but already one of the best. He was also a fine sculptor, much more talented at the work than Tomi would ever be. In the space of a few months, he was already the Master's favorite apprentice. Dre was still away; he had some business in Siena, which meant he would not be home for another fortnight. By day, Tomi and Gio worked on the Baptistery doors, and by night, they patrolled the city streets, restless and uneasy.

Tomi confided in Gio that she was worried about the Red Blood connection and what it might entail. "Perhaps it is time we paid our friend the Changeling a visit," Gio suggested.

The Changeling lived in the sewers of Florence. The creature had not seen daylight in a century, and was shriveled, blind, and wretched. It was too weak to be of any danger to a vampire anymore, and so Andreas had decreed that no one could touch the Croatan, as it was a valuable source of information. In exchange, the Venators let it live.

The Changeling had alerted them to the news that one of its kind had infiltrated the palace guard.

The Changeling was not pleased to see them.

Tomi ignored its hisses and drew a symbol on the cave wall. "We found this mark on a human. Tell us what you know."

Gio prodded the Silver Blood with the tip of his sword. "Answer her, beast, or we shall send you where you belong."

The Changeling laughed. "I do not fear Hell."

"There are worse things than the underworld. Your master is sure to be unhappy with you for forsaking him since Rome. If he has returned, he will exact vengeance on the followers who deserted him," Tomi warned. "Who gave the human the mark? What does it mean?"

Gio battered the creature with a volley of hard blows. "Answer her!"

"I do not know, I do not know!" The Silver Blood cowered. "Only that today, your friend Savonarola was made Cardinal," it said with a crafty smile.

"And?"

"The good friar is a Silver Blood."

"He is lying. Savonarola is no Croatan," Gio scoffed.

Tomi nodded. The Petruvian friar had been a Venator before he entered the clergy.

"He has been Corrupted, turned into Abomination after Trieste," the Changeling told them. In Trieste, the advance team had been attacked by the hive of Silver Bloods they had been tracking. Still, the Venators had won the day—or so Tomi had always believed.

"Who else knows this?" Gio demanded.

"Andreas del Pollaiuolo," the Changeling whispered.

TWENTY-ONE

The Regis Doctrine

*E*ndless meetings. Ever since she'd assumed the title of Regent, Mimi felt as if her life was measured out in marathon conference calls and discussions that went nowhere. Today was a school holiday, some sort of teachers' conference, and in her former life she would have spent the day in the usual comfortable routine: a late brunch followed by a massage, then a leisurely stroll through the boutiques on Madison, stopping only for tea at The Pierre, and then a nap before setting off for dinner at the newest restaurant.

There was no time for such trifles anymore. She spent the day locked in her office, reviewing notes and checking in with her various subcommittees. The Venator team assigned to find Forsyth Llewellyn was the last to check in. While Kingsley's *subvertio* kept Leviathan and Lucifer trapped in the underworld, their co-conspirators were still at large. The Venators reported a tip that put Forsyth in Argentina, and

Mimi agreed to send the team in that direction.

As for Victoria's fate, Mimi was starting to get worried. They were as much in the dark as they had been on day one, and the moon was waning fast. Soon there would be a new moon on the horizon, its first appearance what the Blue Bloods called the shadow crescent—the sliver in the sky that meant a new dawn was at hand.

Since Sunday night there had been no more strange e-mails, but Mimi found the quiet unsettling. Sam and Ted had every Venator in New York on the case, but it might not be enough. Centuries of war had armed her with an inherent understanding of battle strategy, knowledge of armies and combat—but this was a new danger, clever and unpredictable. She was worried the Blue Bloods were too accustomed to their dominance, overly reliant on force and hammer, that they lacked the talent to address kidnapping and subversion.

Mimi put her head in her hands and thought so hard she worried her brain would explode. She had gone through all the books, looking up the history of the Regis, the history of leadership, actions in time of crisis, studying every decision that had been made to bring their Coven here to this moment. Myles Standish (Michael, Pure of Heart) had promised the Blue Bloods they would find safe haven in the new world, and in doing so had broken away from the European Coven. He had invoked the Regis Doctrine to do so. That was it. Mimi could do the same. She could do something if the Venators failed. Of course she could. There was always an answer. She was not helpless. The Code of the Vampires spelled it out in front of her.

The Regis Doctrine: The Regis or Regent must take every precaution to ensure the safety of the Coven by any means necessary.

It gave Mimi an idea. With the power of the Regis Doctrine, she could take down the wards. Why hadn't she thought of it before? It was so simple, really. Whoever had taken Victoria was hiding her physical location, masking her signature in the glom. But with the wards down, every Blue Blood would be visible in the spirit world. It would override any masking spell put upon her, and the Venators would be able to pull Victoria out through the glom.

But it was a risk. The wards that protected the Coven concealed their immortal spirits in the glom and kept the *sangre azul* from the many dangers of the twilight world. Without the wards, they were practically Red Bloods. But it would only be for the briefest moment, Mimi thought—in and out and back again, in the blink of an eye. She would reinstate them the moment they got Victoria back.

She had to try it. If the Venators were unsuccessful, she would take down the wards. She hoped it would not come to that, but if it did, she would be ready. She was not going to let Victoria burn.

Still, even with the danger, Mimi's life went on. Her social life especially. It would not do to miss too many of the usual engagements on her calendar. The Coven would begin to talk, then worry, then panic, and she could not have that. There was enough gossip and agitation as it was, from everything that had happened the month before. She would have to calm the troops, show them there was nothing to worry about. They were still Blue Bloods, the enlightened ones, the blessed and the damned.

Tonight was the opening of an opera at Lincoln Center, and her presence was expected. Mimi turned off her computer. She had to go home and change. In her old life she would have relished the opportunity to wear a hot new dress and show off her jewelry. But now she only felt the dread of obligation. She wanted to be hunting for Victoria, in the Repository with Oliver, or in the glom with the Venators. Not going to some stupid society gala.

After their visit to the blood house, Mimi had decided to follow Committee rules concerning the care of human familiars. She'd located her first familiar, Scott Caldwell, now a senior at NYU, who remembered their affair like it was yesterday and was more than happy to squire her to the event. Scott was just the way she liked her familiars: handsome and dumb, and she hoped his complete inability to process his feelings would mean he would never end up at a blood house after she was done with him. He certainly seemed amenable enough, and looked dashing in a tuxedo.

They walked in, already a bit late, Mimi clutching the train on her ball gown so Scott wouldn't trip on it. She waved to a few familiar faces: the newly bonded Don Alejandro and Danielle Castañeda, who were in from London; there was Muffie Astor Carter, looking serene in blush silk. Helen Archibald, wife to Conclave Elder Josiah Archibald, and one of the Coven's leading matrons, accosted Mimi on her way down the ramp.

"Madeleine, I saw the Taylors yesterday at the ballet. Gertrude looked like hell. She wouldn't tell me, but I heard that something terrible has happened, something to do with that awful video my son showed me. What on earth is going on?"

The Venators had warned Mimi that even after the Conspiracy had taken care of neutralizing the threat of exposure from the video, rumors were swirling that the Silver Bloods were behind it, which was creating rumblings of fear among the older families.

"It's under control," Mimi soothed. "The Conspiracy's taken care of it. A few youthful high jinks, just some of the younger committee members getting creative."

"Well, after what happened at your bonding, maybe disbanding the Coven is something we should consider. Maybe we would be safer . . . not so much a target . . . as before."

"You would have us go into hiding again?" Mimi snapped. "I don't know about you, but I like living aboveground." Since the bonding disaster, there had been whispers among the Coven that perhaps it was time to disband, to go underground. Mimi dismissed it as fearmongering. She had no desire to relive the Dark Ages and was horrified to think that Conclave members would even consider it.

"Spoken like a true dark angel. You don't care about anything but your own convenience," Helen sneered. "You'll put us all in danger. We won't stand for it."

Mimi was shocked. She was aware that not everyone in the Coven was happy to have Azrael as their Regent, and that many would never forget nor forgive her and Abbadon for their part in the revolt against the Almighty. Most probably still blamed them for their banishment. But to throw it in her face like this!

"Excuse me," Mimi said, brushing Helen aside. She'd had enough of the society maven's rudeness. Inside the auditorium the gongs were ringing, reminding guests to take their seats. She followed Scott toward the orchestra doors when her cell phone rang. Oliver calling.

"What is it?" she said testily. "They're about to close the doors and you know they don't do late seating at the Met."

"Don't worry. After you hear what I have to tell you, missing the first act will be the least of your concerns."

Twenty-two

Cabbages and Vines

"I think we might have a lock on Victoria's location," Oliver said grimly. Since their trip to the blood house, he had received permission from Duchesne to miss class and was back to spending all day and night holed up in the Repository, reviewing the tapes, and had finally found a clue as to where she was being kept hostage.

"Ma'am? Will you be joining us?" the usher asked, looking impatient, with his hand on the double doors while Scott fiddled with his cuff links.

"Hold on," she told Oliver, weighing the possibility of whispering into her cell phone while the tenor began his aria. But Trinity had raised her too well. Mimi waved her date inside. "Go ahead, I've got to take this. I'll meet you at intermission."

She walked away from the doors, toward the fountain.

"We've found her?" she asked, pressing the phone to her ear in hopeful anticipation.

"Not yet. But we're on our way."

Mimi glared at the ushers who were shushing her. "Where?"

"The Carlyle Hotel."

"I'll meet you there."

The sidewalk in front of the Carlyle was swarming with Red Bloods. As Mimi walked through the crowd she heard whispers of "bomb threat" and "evacuation." She flashed her Conclave badge to the security team and entered the newly emptied lobby. Oliver was standing with a group of Venators, who had cleared the area by the elevator.

"Sorry about *Parsifal*. It's my favorite opera," he said as a greeting.

"Where is she?" Mimi snapped. She didn't have time for Oliver's clever little commentary right now.

"We think in the penthouse. It's been rented for the month to some actor, but it's been empty for weeks, according to the hotel manager."

"How do you know she's here?"

"We don't. We're just guessing." Oliver pressed the elevator button for the top floor. "I know the Venators are concentrating on those subliminal images, but I thought maybe we should take a closer look at the main video itself. I watched it frame by frame and found something in the shadows. I had tech magnify part of the screen."

He showed her the image on his phone.

"What am I looking at here, exactly?" Mimi asked. It looked like a bunch of squiggles and nothing to get excited about. Certainly not enough to clear an entire hotel lobby and disrupt an evening at the prestigious hotel. Wendell Randolph, the Blue Blood tycoon who owned the Carlyle, was surely going to get annoyed. Mimi saw that she had several messages from him already.

"That's from the wallpaper behind her head. The shine from the Venator rope illuminates it a bit. It's called Cabbage and Vine. It's a famous William Morris design, which went out of production in the 1880s. But when this hotel was built in the 1930s, they had the same textile factory produce it for the hotel. After the renovation last year, only a few rooms kept the original wallpaper. We've already checked the other two. This is the last one."

"We're here because of wallpaper?" Mimi asked. "You guys cleared an entire hotel—used a massive compulsion on all those Red Bloods—because of some wallpaper?" She tried not to sound too incredulous.

"It's all we've got," Oliver said apologetically. "You said no one dies on your watch. We have to try everything, don't we?"

The elevator door opened, and Mimi saw Sam and Ted take position in front of a door to the suite. The rest of the team were arranged in the hallway.

"We have a green?" Ted asked.

Mimi didn't know what to say. At this point they had acted without consulting her, so why adhere to protocol now? It was too late to back out. Maybe it was just courtesy since she had arrived on the scene. It was better than Helen Archibald's rudeness. She would humor her Venators. "Affirmative." She nodded. "Go."

The strike force burst into the room, swarming into the space, setting off glom bombs, their swords held aloft and gleaming.

There was a girl tied up in a chair.

Alas, it was not Victoria.

They had surprised the actor, a movie star, who'd returned the night before with his new girlfriend. At the sight of the black-clad, armored Venators, he dropped a magnum of champagne and fainted.

TWENTY-THREE

The Pub

*A*fter the failure and embarrassment of the Carlyle raid—which Mimi placed directly on Oliver's shoulders to stave off criticism of her Venators— she met the Lennox brothers at their usual pub the next evening. The night was black, and in less than twenty-four hours the crescent moon would appear in the sky. They were almost out of time. She knew the boys wouldn't appreciate what she was about to tell them, but she had no choice. She was Regent now; it was her call. She was not about to lose one of their own. She hoped they had good news for her.

The pub had been a speakeasy during the Prohibition, when the Blue Bloods were the only purveyors of alcohol in the city. The place still had its original double doors, the keyhole to peek out, sawdust on the floor, knotted pine benches scarred with the names of friends and enemies.

Venators of all stripes—jolly veterans with worn faces and cigarettes hanging from their bottom lips, and slim new recruits straight out of Langley (the CIA had been founded by a Venator; the original Blue Bloods training center was located in the same area) jostled at tables next to the odd NYU students who'd wandered in and had no idea they were surrounded by the vampire secret police. There was a pool table and dartboard, and a chalkboard behind the bar for recording rounds.

Mimi found Sam sitting in the back booth surrounded by empties, and took a seat across from him. "It's my shout," Ted announced, bringing back three pints of dark bitter ale topped with a gold lager. Black and Tans they called them. Mimi didn't usually like the taste of beer—she preferred martinis or wine—but she also did not feel like making a fuss. She took a sip. Not too bad, really. Not as tangy as blood—she remembered the taste of Kingsley's blood: sweet and sharp. Her throat constricted and her eyes watered, and for a moment she felt as if she would lose it. But she held herself together.

"First off, take it easy on that Conduit. Hazard-Perry means well," Sam said. "It was as good a guess as any. The kid hasn't slept in days. He works harder than anybody."

"Maybe, but that pompous windbag Wendell Randolph wants my seat for 'abuse of the police force.' He said he's going to call a White Vote at the next meeting."

"He won't. He's all bluster," Ted said with a dismissive

wave. "You're all they've got and they know it."

"Maybe. Look guys, this is hard for me to say." Mimi took a deep breath. "I know we've all worked really hard this last week, and I appreciate all your efforts, but I have no choice: if we don't find her by tomorrow night, I'm taking the wards off the Coven. I don't want to, but it's my only option. I can't have her burn, not online, not anywhere. At least with the wards down we'll know exactly where she is and we'll be able to get her out."

The Venators took the news with sober faces. "That's a huge risk. You know we'd be sitting ducks if the Silver Bloods pulled a stunt at the same time," Ted warned.

"I know the risks." Mimi put her hands in the air. "But do I have a choice?"

"Charles would never allow it," Sam pointed out. "Not even during the slayings," he said, meaning the two years prior when several teenage Blue Bloods were drained.

"Charles let six immortals die," Mimi replied. "And Lawrence lost almost the entire Conclave in Rio. No. I've made up my mind. If we don't find her before midnight, I'm doing it."

Sam pushed back on his chair and put his hands behind his head. Every year of his Enmortal life showed in the creases on his face. "But don't you have got get the full Conclave approval for that sort of thing?"

"Not in a time of war. Not with the Regis Doctrine," said Mimi, a bit smugly. How's that for looking up the Code, she thought. "And gentlemen, if it wasn't clear before, let me make it so. This is a war we're fighting. I'm not going to let security get mired up in useless bureaucratic motions."

Ted exchanged a look with his brother, and Sam shrugged. "All right then, like you said, it's your call, ma'am. But give us until the last minute before you pull the trigger. We've got someone working on a counter to that masking spell. We'll find her. The last time the Regis took the wards off, you remember what happened."

Mimi actually didn't, but she wasn't about to admit that to them, especially after she had already announced her decision. Plus, where did he get off calling her ma'am? "All right. But not one minute more."

"We wanted to show you something too," Sam said. "We got Renfield's notes back. What is wrong with that guy, by the way?"

"He's watched too many movies made by the Conspiracy." Mimi smirked. "Next thing you know he's going to start smelling like roses."

Sam snorted. "He came up with a doozy. Remember those three things we saw on the video?" He began to draw on a cocktail napkin. "Copulating animals. Ram's head. Snake." He tapped the drawing with his pen.

"Uh-huh."

"The scribes found something in the archives—take a look." Sam slid a book across the table. It was an old Repository tome, probably from the 1500s, Mimi guessed, due to the Vitruvian silhouette on the spine. She could smell the dust on it.

Ted opened the book and pointed to an illustration on the left-hand page. It was a symbol divided into three parts. The first showed two interlocking circles, and the second, an animal on four legs. The third symbol was a sword piercing a star.

"Lucifer's sigil," Mimi sighed, pushing the book away. "So this is the Silver Bloods' work after all. Of course."

"Not exactly," Sam said. "It's actually the second symbol that worries us."

"What is it?" Mimi squinted at the image. It looked like a furry little creature of some kind. . . . Like a . . . "It's a lamb, isn't it?"

"Yes."

They didn't have to say anything more. Mimi knew her history as well as they. So that's what the three images on the video meant. They corresponded to the symbols on the tri-glyph: the mating animals stood for union, the ram's head for the sheep, and the snake was yet another symbol for Lucifer. The lamb symbolized humanity. The Red Bloods. A human flock. With Lucifer at its lead. The symbol for union joining the two, lashing them together.

The Silver Bloods were in cahoots with . . . humans? She felt sick. It didn't make sense. Nothing did.

TWENTY-FOUR

The Vanity of Mrs. Armstrong Flood

On Sunday afternoon, Mimi met Oliver at Duchesne. "Are you absolutely certain this is the place this time?" she asked, as they ran up the darkened back stairway.

They had so little time left before the crescent moon rose. This was a farce; she did not even know why she had allowed herself to be talked into this. But if there was a chance to save Victoria without taking down the wards . . . they had to hurry.

When they had arrived at the school, Mimi quickly got them in without setting off any alarms. As Regent, she had the keys and codes to all the Blue Blood strongholds. The dark, empty building had struck her as surprisingly melancholy. She had never been in the school during the off-hours and was surprised to find how quiet and hollow it seemed without its students. She had always thought of Duchesne as a lively place, and now understood that its heart lay in its student body. Without them, the school was just an empty vessel, a stage set.

"I can't have another Carlyle on my hands. Wendell Randolph wants my head on a platter for disrupting his hotel. We had to do a huge memory wipe on all those Red Bloods. Messy. I think the actor wants to sue. He got a scratch on his forehead. His face is insured, you know."

"Actors," Oliver said, as if it were a curse word. "Just get one of the Conspiracy members to give him a part in their new film. I figured we should try everything before you had to take the wards down." He looked out the window at the sky, where the moon was still hidden. "We've got, what . . . fifteen minutes?" he asked, huffing as he led the way.

"Just about." They were cutting it close, but Mimi had promised the Lennox boys they would have every minute until the crescent moon rose, and they had asked her to meet Oliver and give them this one last chance.

It would take an instant to call off the wards. All she had to do was say the words and they would see Victoria immediately. She had made her decision, but now that the time to act was coming upon her, she was starting to have doubts. Should she risk the safety of the entire Coven for the life of one vampire? Charles had never done so, and neither had Lawrence when he was Regis. Why on earth was she Regent? She wasn't ready to make these kinds of decisions! She might be centuries old in blood, but in this cycle she was only seventeen.

Oliver caught his breath for a moment. "Anyway, in answer to your question, we're here because it's one of the places Victoria could be. Sam and Ted are already at the other."

"Other?"

He nodded. "I'll explain in a bit. Remember the Carlyle pattern?"

"Are we back to wallpaper again?" Mimi snapped.

"Hear me out. The pattern on the wallpaper was produced by William Morris in 1880. Its reprint was exclusive to the Carlyle Hotel. No one else in the world is supposed to have that wallpaper. But it kept bothering me—why did that pattern look so familiar? I thought I'd seen it before, and not just at the Carlyle."

"Okay."

"Then I did some digging up on the history of the hotel. Did you know it was owned by the Floods? The same family who gave their mansion to the Duchesne School. Mrs. Flood—Rose—was a leading tastemaker back in the day. It wasn't unreasonable to assume she had picked out that wallpaper personally. It took a lot of trouble to reproduce it—they practically had to buy the factory that did it. And so it got me thinking—if she loved it so much—maybe . . ."

"She put it in her bedroom," Mimi finished. "Victoria's in the attic, then? All this time?"

"That's my guess. Or in their Newport mansion, which is where the boys are. It's a museum now, so I thought it was best if we took this place and sent them there. That way you don't have to answer to the Preservation Society of Newport if things get messy, like they did the other day."

"Good thinking, but you know if you're wrong, I'm having your memory wiped and you'll never work for us again."

"Promise?"

Mimi and Oliver flew up the stairs to Mrs. Flood's bedroom. The top-floor classrooms had been abandoned several years ago, after too many of the Red Blood students swore they had seen or heard ghosts. Silly humans, there was no such thing as ghosts! Only apparitions set off by vampires fooling around in the glom. But in order to appease the human population, the area had been sealed off by the administration. It did make for a good place to hide someone, since the distraction spell kept the area clear of humans while the vampires chalked up any strange activity as consequence to the spell. But to think that all along, Victoria had been here—just underneath their noses—was almost insulting. It was if whoever had done this was taunting them.

Mimi pressed her ear against the door. She could hear something—a terrible grunting noise and a shuffling. She pushed against the door. It was held by a massive blocking spell. Crap. Spellcasting and unmaking were not her areas of expertise, aside from that one time when she had dabbled in the Dark Arts.

"Try an exploder," Oliver suggested.

"I am," Mimi said, annoyed that she hadn't thought

of it earlier. She focused on the doorknob and visualized it disintegrating into nothingness, blasting open, and allowing her inside.

The doorknob shook and shivered but the door remained locked. The terrible grunting noise grew louder, accompanied by a fearful, low moaning. Victoria? What was happening behind the door? Mimi's heart began to pump. She could feel waves of fear emanating from behind the doorway.

She tried again and shook her head. Whatever was holding it was strong. It was like ramming into a cement wall. "It's jammed up hard," she grunted. She looked outside the window. It was almost dark. The sky was the color of gray sand—the first hint of light on the horizon. The crescent moon would soon show its face.

"She's in there," Oliver urged, his shoulder pushing on the door as if that would help.

Mimi was about to answer, but before she could, from inside the room came a scream so terrible that she forgot everything she was doing. In an instant, she made her decision. There was no more time to waste. Victoria was going to burn.

She had to take the wards down. Now.

Azrael stepped into the glom, the mighty and terrible Angel of Death, a white queen wielding a dark sword flashing with the light of the heavens. Her six-foot wings stretched to their full span.

She said the words only Michael had said before her.

The wards fell, and in an instant the glom was filled with the spirits of every living vampire, and Mimi saw, through the jumble of souls, one particular girl screaming in the corner—a girl whose spirit had been, until now, hidden from the Coven—

Victoria!

In the glom, Mimi saw Sam and Ted Lennox moving toward Victoria, reaching for her—coming at her from the other side.

Then, for some inexplicable reason, the Venators looked up and turned away from Victoria and began running toward Mimi—their identical faces frozen in utter horror.

What are you doing? No . . . go back . . . Vix . . .

Mimi was so close, close enough to reach for Victoria's hand. Their fingers brushed against each other's in the twilight—

But before she could pull Victoria out into the real world, something hit Mimi with the magnitude of a firebomb, and it felt as though every atom in her body exploded out of existence.

TWENTY-FIVE

Crescent Moon

hen Mimi blinked open her eyes, she was lying on the floor, covered in sawdust. A familiar face hovered above hers. She coughed. Whatever had hit her, it *hurt*. She felt as if she had cracked three ribs and inhaled a wall of asbestos. She was surprised to find she was still alive— she felt as if she had been pulled apart in a million pieces only to be stitched up again. What was that? A blood spell? It had to be. What else would knock her out like that, and in the glom? But if it was a blood spell, how was she still here?

"What happened?" she choked, realizing she was now inside the attic bedroom. The door was lying open and broken on the floor next to her. She looked around—Oliver had been right: the room was plastered with the same wallpaper from the original video. The same intricate pattern. There was a chair in the middle of the room, and Venator rope was tangled at its feet. A video camera was set up right across from it. This was where Victoria had been filmed. But she wasn't here anymore. How had they been able to move her without unmasking her glom signature?

"Where is she? Where's Victoria?" she croaked.

In answer, Oliver shakily pointed to a flickering computer monitor on a desk in the middle of the empty room.

On the screen, Victoria Taylor was burning to death. Melting into the black flames. Her vampire skin was scorched and peeling, the blood turning obsidian as it was destroyed forever.

Victoria was in the Newport house. The Lennox brothers popped out of the glom, and they tried valiantly to fight the flames, but it was too late. Nothing could stop hellfire from burning once it began to consume the immortal spirit it was set to destroy.

"Goddamnit!" Sam Lennox cried, kicking at the burning chair, while his brother wept beside him.

Mimi fell to the floor, her knees buckling beneath her. She remembered: the glom, Victoria, the Venators. They had been so close. The Venators could have saved Victoria, but at the final second, the Lennoxes had turned away to try to save Mimi instead. They had seen the blood spell headed in her direction. Now they were too late. They were all too late. She had put the entire Coven in danger, she had almost been killed—and for what? She had been unable to save Victoria, just as she had been unable to save Kingsley. "Oh God."

In the end, there was nothing left of Victoria but a pile of ashes.

Mimi buried her face in her hands and sobbed. She had failed so wretchedly. She was useless. As good as a Silver Blood. Worse.

Oliver quietly shut down the computer.

Outside, the crescent moon was high in the sky, shining in its silver glory.

The Cardinal

If the Changeling was to be believed, Andreas had allowed a Silver Blood to take control of the human church. Surely Andreas could not have known. He would never allow such blasphemy. Unless . . . unless Andreas was not who Tomi thought he was. Unless he was not Michael. Unless he was not her beloved. Tomi did not know what or who to believe anymore. This had never happened before. She could always recognize her twin in every incarnation, and every fiber of her being told her Michael was Andreas. How could she be so wrong? She could not understand it. There had to be another explanation. She could not accept it. And yet . . .

"Andreas is a traitor. I felt it, but I did not want to speak until I was sure," Gio said, articulating every doubt Tomi held in her mind.

It was midday, and the newly inducted Cardinal was receiving a line of visitors wishing to kiss his ring and congratulate him on his newly elevated position. As Venators, they skipped the line and were quickly escorted inside his private office by his secretary.

"My friends!" Savonarola greeted Gio and Tomi with open arms.

Gio wasted no time. As soon as they entered, he reached and grabbed the priest by the neck. He squeezed the Cardinal's throat until the man could not breathe. Savonarola's eyes turned silver with crimson pupils.

"Abomination!" Gio spat. "You were an angel once," he said, motioning to the view and the world that the Blue Bloods had built—a glorious city of beauty, peace, love, and light. "We will not allow you to destroy what we have made."

"Where is your master? Where is he hiding?" Tomi demanded.

The Cardinal only cackled, but his secretary—a human Conduit hovering by the door—provided the answer. Trembling with fear, he told them, "He is in the highest tower, in the home of the Mistress—" But before he was able to finish his sentence, Savonarola burst away from the Venator's hold, grabbed a jeweled dagger from his desk, and stabbed the human to death.

"I was promised no harm would come to me!" the Cardinal cried, as Gio's sword slashed his neck, beheading the Silver Blood priest.

PART THE THIRD

DEMING CHEN, MERCY-KILLER

New York

The Present

TWENTY-SIX

An Angel Descends

"As many of you know, two weeks ago, in an attempt to save Victoria Taylor, I chose to remove the wards that guard our Coven for a very brief period. However, we were unable to retrieve her in time, as I myself was attacked by a blood spell in the glom." The young Regent looked over the assembled Venators and Conclave members with sad eyes. Her voice was grave. "I survived the more insidious effects of the spell, but Victoria was not so lucky. She was murdered."

The room remained silent for a long time. No one spoke or made any kind of noise: no nervous coughing, no impatient scraping of a chair. From her seat in the back, Deming Chen watched the Blue Bloods carefully. She was impressed by their ability to hold their emotions in check, but she sensed fear and anger from the assembled group.

This was not a good sign. It meant as Regent, Mimi Force

did not have the backing of her Conclave. It was a pity, as anyone who could deflect a blood spell without a mark on her must have had very powerful protection at her disposal, and was worthy of respect and admiration. When Mimi had first gotten in touch with her, Deming was shocked to find that the rumors were true, that the New York Coven was being led by someone so early in her cycle, and carried the spirit of Azrael, no less. Things really must be dire if the Coven had the Angel of Death at its head. Deming had met Mimi Force only once before, during the Four Hundred Ball almost two years ago, when the newborn flock revealed their immortal identities.

Deming liked Mimi well enough, although the memory of the Blue Bloods' long-ago insurrection was still sharp in her mind, as if it had happened yesterday. Azrael and Abbadon had led the campaign against the Almighty—had helped the Morningstar assemble a legion of the best and brightest. *We are the gods now*, Azrael had told them. *The rule of Paradise can be ours.* The great and mighty warrior queen had flattered and persuaded them, had convinced them they had been chosen personally for their strengths. How could they refuse?

Deming looked around: this was a sorry group indeed, filled with the elderly and the untested. Some of the Conclave members looked like they were way past the time for their cycle to be over, while some, like the Regent, were only coming into their full powers and memories. Not that she should be so critical, as she herself had just celebrated her seventeenth birthday.

That the Blue Blood ranks had been reduced to such a state was troubling, to say the least. News was bad all over: the European Coven was in a communication blackout after what had happened in Paris; they refused to send word or share information, fearing other traitors in the community. In South America, the Conclave had declared martial law, and inter-Coven transactions shut down. Deming had expected more from the North American delegation—New York was famously the most powerful stronghold of the vampires. This was where Michael and Gabrielle had made their home. But the Uncorrupted had disappeared to who knows where, and no one knew when and if they would ever return. The vampires were on their own.

Deming drained her coffee cup. It had been an eighteen-hour flight into Kennedy Airport from Pudong, and she had spent the entire time poring over the Venator reports, re-reading every log, scrutinizing every decision. The Truth Seekers had operated by the book, and she could not find fault in their actions, but this junction required more from them than routine operations. She tried to hide a yawn. She had barely slept and could feel a giant headache forming. You'd think as immortals they would be immune from jet lag, she thought ruefully.

At the front of the room, the Regent was calling her name, and she realized with a start that everyone was looking at her. "Please allow me to introduce Venator Deming Chen. Time and again, Deming has proven to be one of our most effective and efficient Truth Seekers. I'm sure many of you remember that she, along with her twin, Dehua, was instrumental during critical victories in our history: the Egyptian Terrors, the Crisis in Rome, and the Monumental Schism are only a few of the battles her sword has helped us win. We are grateful that her Coven was kind enough to send her to help us on this case."

That was quite an introduction, akin to reading a résumé, really, but Deming was used to it. As Kuan Yin, Angel of Mercy, she was highly sensitive to emotion and mood, and back in Shanghai was famous for her talent at reading a person's *guānghuán* or, in the Sacred Language, *affectus*, the color representation of one's interior barometer that was undetectable to the eye. She was one of two vampires (her sister was the other) who could see it without the help of the glom. Red Bloods had a name for it as well, but those charlatans who purported to read a person's "aura" were doing nothing but guesswork. You had to have angel sight to be able to read the real thing.

Deming stood and joined Mimi at the podium. "Six months ago, a vampire from our Coven was kidnapped," she said, taking a remote control from the table and pulling up two photographs on the back screen. It showed Victoria, tied and blindfolded on one side, and a dark-haired girl bound in a similar manner on the other.

"Liling Tang's father is one of the richest men in China, and Liling's abductors demanded twenty million dollars for her release. Because of the money issue, naturally we concentrated on the humans in our community. However, in the end, we discovered she was taken by one of us. A Blue Blood."

The assembled group did not stir. It was almost as if they had expected it, and Deming soldiered on. "Her location was hidden by a masking spell, but after a thorough investigation, we were able to figure out where she was being held, and rescued her before the appointed deadline."

She continued. "I've gone over Victoria's file. According to the Warden overseers, Victoria arrived at the party at eleven p.m. After that she was never seen anywhere again. Otherwise the Wardens would have picked up on her glom signature when she left. Therefore, whoever took her was at that party, which means whoever did this was someone close to her as well—someone from her inner circle. Someone from Duchesne. Someone she trusted."

"Deming will be enrolled as a senior at Duchesne," the Regent announced. "She will infiltrate Victoria Taylor's close group of friends, those who had been at Jamie Kip's party on the night in question. As we do not want to cause unnecessary fear or panic, this must remain a strict undercover operation."

"I've got a question. How did you find Liling if her glom signature was masked?" Ted Lennox asked. Deming had met him the night before; he had picked her up at the airport with his brother.

"We sent a DeathWalker into the glom."

The room buzzed at this information. "A glom-induced coma? To hide the spirit trail? But the potential damage to the soul is . . ." Ted shook his head. "You'd have to be really crazy or really brave to do something like that. Who'd you find to carry out such a risky operation?"

"I did it myself," Deming said coolly. It was either her or Dehua, and Deming had always been the stronger of the twins. She hadn't allowed her sister to take the risk.

The crowd murmured its approval. DeathWalkers stripped their immortal spirit to its very essence, and in doing so mimicked death. With no trace of her spirit in the glom, she had been able to go underneath the masking spell and find the physical location of the hostage.

The Regent tapped her lectern. "Are there any more questions?" She looked around. There were none. "I don't have to remind you that this information is classified to the Conclave and the Venator team originally assigned to the case. No one else in the Coven must know we are conducting an internal investigation. As far as they are concerned, the Conspiracy has taken care of the security breach posed by the online video. The mainstream world remains blissfully ignorant of our existence. Victoria's disappearance has been explained as a transfer to a Swiss boarding school. The Taylors have been alerted to the situation and are cooperating."

The meeting ended, and as Deming collected her things, the Regent walked to her side. Deming was struck by Azrael's beauty. It was said among the vampires that only Gabrielle was lovelier, although it had been a while since Deming had seen her in the flesh. Deming had not been in cycle when Allegra was still active. The Regent's translucent skin had the creamy freshness of youth, a radiant vitality in contrast to heavy sadness in her emerald green eyes. "You have everything you need?" Mimi asked. "How are the boys treating you?"

"Venator quarters are a dump. Just like back home." Deming grinned. "But I'll manage."

"Glad to hear. Remember, at school, I don't know you. So please don't take anything I do or say personally."

"I'll try to keep that in mind," said Deming. She made for the door, but she got the sense that the Regent still had something she wanted to say, so she stuck around.

Mimi waited until the room was completely empty to speak. "There's another thing. It's come to my attention that there are those among us who believe that as community we pose too much of a target. Venators loyal to me have discovered that Josiah Archibald and several other Conclave members are planning a coup to disband the Coven. They're going to shut down the Repository, move the House of Records underground, and take half of the registered families with them. I've let them think I don't know anything about their plans. But I need to find the killer. If I can figure out who's behind the videos, I can regain their trust, calm the opposition, and make the Coven whole again."

Deming nodded. Mimi had not mentioned this when she'd debriefed her on the assignment, and it was a shock to learn the New York Coven was in such jeopardy. But then, no other Coven had lost as many immortal lives. "The blood spell that hit you—do you think the Conclave had something to do with it?" Deming asked.

"The Venators aren't completely certain yet; they're still breaking down the mechanics of the spell. But right now it's our best guess that yes, it was intended to get me out of the way." Mimi bowed her head. "The Conclave had access to my Repository log. Somehow they found out I was planning to take down the wards."

"Do you think they were involved in Victoria's abduction?"

"No. Of course not. But they used it as an opportunity to attack me."

"Can I ask how you deflected the blood spell?"

The Regent sighed. "I'm not sure myself. As far as our doctors can tell, it just passed through me—neutralized on impact. As if I were wearing a bulletproof vest."

"Whatever it was, you were very lucky. I've seen victims of blood spells. It's not pretty," Deming said, sparing Mimi the details: the scraping of remains, the consequent blood burning that was a mercy, since the immortal spirit had been blasted into nothingness. Blood spells were nasty little devices, a way to harness the glom and unleash its effects on one person, targeting the molecules in the vampire's blood. "Anyway, Coven disbandment seems a rather radical proposition," she observed.

"They're trying to get rid of me because they know I would never allow it," the Regent said, looking up with her eyes bright. "Every vampire for himself? No more cycle births? Don't they remember what it was like before? If Charles was here they would never even attempt something like this."

"Don't worry, I'll find your killer," Deming said, putting a hand on Mimi's arm.

"Good." The Regent had a covetous look on her that Deming didn't fully understand until she realized that Mimi was jealous of her. Jealous that Deming had been able to save her hostage, whereas Mimi had fallen short—and as punishment, her Coven's very foundation was imperiled. It was surely not what she had wanted to accomplish when she had removed the wards.

"It wasn't your fault, what happened to Victoria," Deming said. "You shouldn't blame yourself. Don't worry. I won't fail. I never have."

Mimi shook her hand. "Make sure that you don't. What the Elders don't realize is that if they succeed in disbanding us . . . there is a very real possibility that we will never rise again."

TWENTY-SEVEN

The New Girl

*T*he room she had been assigned was a small one that faced the shaft, so that the window opened to a view of a brick wall, five feet away. In Shanghai she had command of a top-floor penthouse, although pollution in the city was so bad she almost had the same view there as here: a gray darkness. The Lennox brothers, who lived on the top floor, had offered their help, but she had refused them for now. She worked better alone.

Deming grabbed her bag and left the building, planning on taking the subway uptown. The pressure on her to deliver was intense, but she savored the challenge. There was nothing she liked more than a zero endgame, especially since she had no intention of losing. Colleagues in Shanghai had called the Chen twins arrogant, but she didn't see it that way. The twins were different from the rest. Like the legendary Kingsley Martin, they did whatever it took to get results.

They were cold and ruthless, and would stop at nothing to get to the truth. Which was why the Coven had felt comfortable in sending one of them to New York, since they got to keep the other.

This was her third embed mission since becoming a Venator a year ago (she and Dehua had taken advantage of the new rules regarding recruitment, and like the Force twins, had joined up early), and she prepared herself mentally for the day to come. Until Liling Tang's abduction, the Asian Coven's biggest headache had been human rights abuses—too many vampires draining their familiars to full consumption and leaving a trail of Red Blood corpses in their wake, or else using memory wipes a little too liberally, so that humans became mentally impaired. Right now her sister was in the rural countryside, tracking down a *probrae spiritus*, a vampire who was using the glom to give the local human population nightmares.

The Duchesne assignment was more akin to what they had pulled at the International School, when they had been brought in on the kidnapping case. Liling Tang had run around with a sophisticated expatriate crowd, shunning the usual clique of rich kids from the Communist aristocracy. Her friends had been Blue Bloods from around the world, and her kidnapper a European transfer. The crime had caused the Chinese Conclave to consider seceding from the global vampire community, but so far they had elected to remain loyal to New York.

Deming was well aware that Duchesne was unlike your typical American high school—there were no cheerleaders prancing about in tiny skirts that barely covered their behinds, no hulking football players stalking the hallways, no show choir geeks, no threat of slushie facials (perhaps she had just watched too much American television), but the moment she stepped through its ornate double doors, she found it was just like everywhere else.

There was a rigid separation of the wheat from the chaff, the cool from the dorky, the beautiful from the not. The popular kids, Victoria's friends among them, congregated in the outdoor courtyard before the first bell: the girls with enviable figures, sleek hair and blinding teeth, holding giant Parisian tote bags as backpacks, surrounded by handsome boys, tousled and dreamy-looking, their jackets and ties askew, as if they had rolled up to school straight from bed. This was the in-crowd, the charmed circle, the Blue Bloods—this was the group Deming was meant to join.

It shouldn't be too hard, Deming thought. She did not have any false modesty about her looks: she knew she was pretty, with her straight black hair that fell all the way down her back, coffee-colored skin, her wide eyes and button nose, her slim boyish build. Plus, she had a lot of experience being "the New Girl." Her cycle father was an industrialist with many holdings all over the world, and the twins had been educated in London, Tehran, Johannesburg, and Hong

Kong. She knew how to get along with people, how to make them like her.

All Committee meetings, Junior and Senior, were postponed for the time being, as the Wardens were too busy strengthening the wards around the Coven after the Regent's impulsive action. No one even knew how badly the Regent had exposed them to their enemies and what the repercussions would be. No wonder the Conclave had lost its faith in its leader. No wonder the future of the Coven was on the brink.

It was too bad the meetings had been canceled indefinitely. It would have been an easy way to mingle with the group without being noticed. Deming looked at her schedule. Her first class was The Spirit of the Self, a humanities elective for upperclassmen. Whoever had planned the school's curriculum was certainly given to alliteration: she could have taken Debating Decisions (ethics), Movement and Motion (a dance class), or From Barriers to Bridges (an English class, to Deming's surprise). Whatever happened to plain old History or Algebra or Art?

She had chosen the class because three of her top suspects were enrolled as well, and took a seat next to Francis Kernochan, whom everyone called Froggy, one of the two boys last seen with Victoria Taylor at Jamie Kip's party. Froggy certainly didn't look like someone keeping a terrible secret. The boy had an open, amiable face, hair an unfortunate shade of orange, and from the slouch of his rounded shoulders alone, an easygoing demeanor. Not that it meant anything. The Blue Blood boy from Guizhou who had drained twenty-four familiars to death had the face of an angel.

"Excuse me," she said, as her messenger bag brushed the elbow of the girl seated on her other side.

"Are those chopsticks?" the girl asked. Deming looked up to see a pretty strawberry blonde sizing her up. Piper Crandall. Suspect Number Two. As Victoria's best friend, she was the one who would have the most reason to harm the girl. In Deming's experience, it was always those closest to us who also wished us dead.

"That's so cool," Piper told her.

"Thanks." Deming's hand reflexively went to pat the long black hair she wore in a messy bun on the top of her head, secured with elegant sterling-silver chopsticks, the current trend in Shanghai. They weren't any old chopsticks either: they had been forged by the master, Alalbiel, and when joined together they formed her sword, *Ren Ci Sha Shou*, Mercy-Killer.

"I love your watch," she said, pointing to Piper's wrist. "Is it vintage?"

"An original Cartier, from when Louis still made them." Piper smiled. "Funny how Red Bloods think you can't take it with you. I've had this watch for almost two hundred years."

"It's gorgeous," said Deming, who didn't need to use the glom to know the road to female friendship was paved with flattery. Why use the glom when common sense and insight into human (and vampire) behavior was available? Too many Truth Seekers had become lazy and dependent on telepathic tricks. They had lost the ability to think without them.

"Maybe I'll let you borrow it sometime if you teach me how to wear my hair that way," Piper said.

"Anytime," Deming said. "I'm Deming Chen." As part of her cover she had rolled into Duchesne wearing the latest fashions, and noticed Piper looking approvingly at her expensive handbag.

"Piper Crandall. I know who you are. We got the Conclave memo that you had transferred here. Where are you staying?"

"My uncle's a Venator and he has some rooms on Bleecker."

"Tragic." Piper shook her head. "They haven't fixed up that place since like . . ."

"The nineteenth century," they chorused together.

Piper laughed. "That place is probably as old as my watch. If you get tired of staying there, come hang out at my house. We have TiVo. I bet those old-timers don't even have a TV."

A promising start, Deming thought. After a few days of tedious, diligent friendship with Piper Crandall—the usual borrowing of each other's clothes and gossiping about boys—she planned to get to the bottom of what exactly happened to Victoria Taylor on the night of Jamie Kip's birthday party.

Twenty-eight

Dark Angel

iper Crandall was from one of the most solid families of the New York Coven, and her immortal background was immaculate. The Crandalls were Van Alen loyalists. Piper's cycle grandparents had been two of Cordelia and Lawrence Van Alen's closest allies on the Conclave. Their fortunes in the Coven had risen at the same time that Lawrence had been named Regis.

Under the guise of friendship, Deming had been able to undertake a comprehensive scan on Piper's subconscious without the vampire suspecting anything. So far, Piper gave every indication of being nothing but a normal, well-rounded Blue Blood.

Deming hoped to probe deeper into the tangled layers of her memory. There were many ways to hide the truth, even from oneself, but sooner or later surface innocence revealed the dark heart of guilt. But if Piper was responsible for Victoria's death, Deming still had to find a motive. That was the prickly thing—even if Piper secretly hated Victoria, she had to have a reason to kill her. Something that sent the pendulum swinging from closet animosity to outright violence. Victoria's demise was calculated and cruel, and if Piper had a hand in it, she had to have had good reason to do so. Deming had her theories, mostly along the lines of how girlish affection had masked a bitter rivalry and resentment. She had seen girls kill their friends for less, but so far nothing about Piper indicated that she had been anything other than fond of Victoria.

Another puzzle was the nature of the video: if Piper or another one of Victoria's friends had done this, why did they seek to expose the vampires as well?

That afternoon, she followed Piper into their shared seminar. As Deming understood it, The Spirit of the Self was an excuse for these overprivileged children to read books and watch old movies and pontificate on philosophical matters of which they had no understanding so they could cruise into an easy A that pumped up their transcripts. (The class did not have a final exam, only two term papers.) If Deming found it all too precious, it was a welcome change after an earlier embed assignment. A few months ago, she'd had to go undercover as a factory worker in a sweatshop to gather evidence that its Blue Blood owners were using compulsion to drive their Red Blood workers to the brink of exhaustion.

The professor, a long-haired ex-hippie, began the lesson.

"So how did you all like *Paradise Lost?*" he asked. Yesterday they had watched the movie *The Devil's Advocate*. The theme of this year's seminar was the depiction of evil in the modern world, the devil as a pop-culture commodity.

"I hated it," a boy answered immediately. "Milton makes the devil into Heathcliff with a pitchfork. He makes evil too seductive." He was slim and shy-looking, with curly dark hair and bright blue eyes. Paul Rayburn was a merit aid student, one of the Red Blood kids allowed to enroll at a reduced tuition. He probably had no idea he was surrounded by immortals. In Shanghai they called such humans *sheep*, and Deming was not interested in sheep.

"I disagree. I don't see Lucifer as a monster. I think he's merely misunderstood. I mean, without him, there's no story, right?" asked another dark-haired boy. This one was slumped in his seat, a pen in his mouth. His thick dark hair was brushed away from his forehead to reveal piercing dark eyes. There was something about his face that was more arresting and striking than handsome, and there was something twisted about his mouth that made him look like he would enjoy watching innocent creatures die.

So this was Suspect Number Three: Bryce Cutting. A dark angel, Deming realized, from his *affectus* alone. The Venator reports had failed to mention that. While there were certainly a number from the Underworld who had pledged to follow Michael and Gabrielle upon Exile, there were not many. Deming did not want to be prejudiced against his provenance—it made her as silly as a Red Blood with their obsessions about race (like many Blue Bloods Deming had lived in many different cycles under a multitude of ethnicities)—but it was still something to consider. There were very few dark angels around who had not gone Silver Blood. Bryce Cutting, like the current Regent, was one of them.

"Interesting point, Bryce." Their professor nodded. "Satan's story does propel the narrative."

Bryce gave his adversary a smug grin, but it only inveighed a passionate response from Paul. "But that's exactly why the story blows—the devil recast as romantic hero. I can't stomach that Satan's desire to be godlike is sympathetic. We shouldn't root for evil," he argued. "The whole idea of idealizing jealousy and ambition is just like how *Wall Street* became a huge advertisement for getting rich off the stock market rather than the scathing polemic Oliver Stone had intended. Instead of the audience hating Michael Douglas, they wanted to be him. Greed is good, and they loved it. It's the same here. The devil is us, and we're supposed to relate to the scale of his ambition? What was wrong with staying in Paradise? Was playing a lyre and flying around in the clouds really so bad? I don't think so." Paul smiled.

The class tittered, and Paul seemed to win the debate, but Bryce had no intention of conceding the point. "Tragic hero is right. This country was founded on the same idea that the story is based on—that it's better to rule in Hell than serve in Heaven. Better to be independent, and the master of your own universe, than a slave," Bryce said triumphantly.

Paul scoffed. "I don't think the Founding Fathers had *Paradise Lost* in mind when they drafted the Constitution."

"How do you know?" Bryce asked. "You weren't there."

For a moment, Deming wondered if Bryce would reveal his immortal status and bare his fangs to scare the poor human to death. Of course Bryce was just being deliberately argumentative, and in any event, he had a poor grasp of American history (Deming would bet he had not been in cycle during the time). Most likely, it irked him that Paul had unknowingly stumbled upon the truth. John Milton, one of the members of the original Conspiracy, had written the poem to warn humanity of the devil's temptations, and instead, the Red Bloods had taken to it as a tragic story of unfulfilled promise. She suspected Bryce was annoyed that Paul, a lowly human with a sharp mind and the ability to sway opinions, had gained popularity in the class.

Still, it was blasphemy for any Blue Blood to talk in such a manner about the Morningstar. Lucifer a hero? Merely misunderstood? Of course she had heard New York was a very liberal Coven, but still. She had been concentrating her efforts on cracking Piper, but maybe there wasn't anything in that pretty head of hers but the usual teenage angst and drama. Deming had not yet been ready to give up on her, but with those words, Bryce Cutting just jumped to the front of the line.

TWENTY-NINE

New Rules

ater that afternoon, Deming counted a dozen
kids from Bryce's crowd crammed into two
pushed-together tables in the back of the local pizza par-
lor. This being the Upper East Side, the place looked more
like an art gallery than a casual neighborhood hangout, with
a grand domed glass ceiling above the dining room, overlooking a sweeping view of the park.

Right in the middle of the festive group was Mimi Force,
but as the Regent had warned, she gave Deming no indication
that she recognized her, and didn't even glance in her direction. Deming found a place between Croker "Kiki" Balsan
and Bozeman "Booze" Langdon (did they all have such silly
names?) and directed her attention at the conversation.

Daisy Foster, a fellow senior, was talking about Victoria's
abrupt departure. "Ugh, Vix is so lucky. The European
Coven lets them do anything. Have you seen the latest rules

from the Committee? Now we have to register prospective familiars for blood tests and psychology profiles before they 'allow' us to have them. It's crazy!" she said, picking up a slice of pizza and taking a tiny bite. "Who has the time?"

"It's for our own good," Mimi said, shaking her empty Diet Coke can. "Only a certain kind of Red Blood makes a good familiar. There are a lot of risks, and diseases can be inconvenient and costly. The Wardens really should have done this before."

Daisy scoffed. "Until you got all fancy-schmancy on us, you were the worst offender, Mimi. I mean, how many familiars have you had? None of them are registered, I'll bet."

"Yeah, why don't you tell us about what really goes on in the Conclave? I mean, is Vix really in Switzerland?" Willow Frost cackled.

Mimi responded mildly. "I got an e-mail from her the other day. She's spending spring break in Gstaad. We can meet her there if we want."

"She never said anything about a ski trip! Since when were you guys so close?" Piper blurted, looking a bit hurt. If the girl had done her best friend harm, she certainly knew how to hide it, Deming thought.

"That Vix," Stella Van Rensslaer said. "I can't believe she didn't even let us throw her a good-bye party. She just up and left! And whatever happened to her little boyfriend? We never see him around anymore. Don't you think it's weird? How the two of them are gone all of a sudden? Remember what happened with Aggie Carondolet and all those people a couple years ago? I bet the Conclave's hiding something."

"Well, someone *could* tell us, but won't," Piper accused, looking directly at Mimi.

"I told you guys, it's an honorary title. They don't actually let me *do* anything. I mean, c'mon," Mimi protested. "They just gave it to me because Charles has been gone so long. The Conclave makes all the decisions. I don't even get invited to meetings."

Deming thought it was smart of Mimi to not let her peers understand the breadth of her newfound powers and responsibility. For one, they wouldn't believe it anyway, since she was so young. And two, some in the Coven might be uncomfortable to know the extent of her influence. While Azrael and Abbadon were two of the Blue Bloods' fiercest and strongest fighters, their power had always been held in check by the Uncorrupted. With Michael and Gabrielle missing, this was a whole different scenario. No wonder the Conclave was planning a coup d'etat.

Froggy tossed a bread stick in Bryce's direction, and an epic bread stick fight broke out between the boys, with the girls laughing and screaming for them to stop—they were getting garlic in their hair.

Deming noticed the rest of the customers were looking at their table with sour expressions. The vampires were making a spectacle of themselves, drawing attention. They were acting just like Red Bloods. Foolish and careless. Deming caught Mimi's eyes, but the Regent looked resigned.

Outside, Mimi sent, and excused herself from the table. A few minutes later, after paying her portion of the check, Deming followed her to a back alley behind the restaurant, where they would not be seen by the rest of the group.

"You're supposed to check in with me every morning. What've you got so far?" Mimi asked. "The rats in the Conclave already have the scribes dismantling the Repository. How can they think I don't notice?" She shook her head in disbelief.

"I'm still getting in with them. It's only been three days," Deming said. "There hasn't been anything to file yet. It takes a while to break these things."

The Regent tugged on a lock of her hair nervously. "My sources tell me they're planning to go in a fortnight. They're going to take over headquarters and lock me and the Venators out."

"There's nothing you can do?"

"I can't show my hand until I can give them the killer. It's the only way to keep the Coven together and convince them to stay."

"I'll have your killer before then."

Mimi hugged herself tightly. "You'd better. Keep me posted on your progress." She left to join the group, who were now congregated on the sidewalk, and after a few minutes, Deming did too.

"We're headed to Stella's," Piper said, upon seeing the

Venator. "Her brother is home from Brown and he has the most adorable friends."

"Not me," Deming replied a little abruptly. Her impromptu meeting with the Regent had annoyed her. All right, she had to act faster, did she? She looked over to the group of boys horsing around by tossing Froggy's iPhone between them.

She said good-bye to the girls and walked over to Bryce. "Walk me home?" she asked, barreling her way through the crowd.

Bryce looked her over. They had spent the last couple of days hanging out in the same crowd of people but had not exchanged two words to each other until this minute. Not that it mattered, really, as long as he fancied her, and Deming had never had a boy turn her down yet. "Sure, why not," he said, as she knew he would. His voice was like Tabasco and honey: hoarse and sweet at the same time. "Catch you guys later," he told his friends, as he and Deming walked away.

Deming studied the handsome boy at her side. She had seen a lot of injustice and cruelty in her time as a Venator, and careless disregard for life offended her deeply. She did not care if it was an immortal or mortal one, each life was valuable. Had Bryce Cutting decided that Victoria's was not? And if so, why?

She'd promised the Regent she would find Victoria's murderer. Deming had not yet made a promise she couldn't keep.

THIRTY

The Girlfriend Role

*D*ating Bryce was almost too easy. After he'd walked her home from the pizza place, they were immediately an item. The next day at school he was already waiting for her after each class so they could make out in the hallways. She was still getting used to the taste of his tongue in her throat and having to answer to "Babe."

Now it was a Saturday afternoon, and the boys were indulging in their usual post–crew practice ritual: video games and lounging. Bryce had invited her to meet him at Froggy's town house. When she arrived she immediately excused herself to the powder room upstairs but crept into Froggy's bedroom instead. In the time it would take Red Blood agents to dust a fingerprint, she had already performed a thorough survey of Froggy's immediate surroundings and family background.

She had downloaded a copy of his hard drive to send to

tech, and performed a test in the glom to see if she could find any clue in the spirit memory. If he had been the culprit, she would have been able to detect traces of guilt, horror, or violence in his immediate physical surroundings. Especially if he had been handling devil flame, which left a distinctive smell years after it had burned out—the fire in Rio was still smoldering. But the only thing she could detect was a malodorous waft from the laundry basket containing his socks.

She sighed as she slid back Froggy's bureau drawer. Just as she'd suspected, there was nothing extraordinarily good or terrible about the boy, who carried the spirit of a minor angel with a rather uneventful history. As for his cycle parents, the Kernochans had almost no interest in Coven business. Neither of them had ever served as an Elder or a Warden; they were apolitical types who wouldn't be able to fight a Silver Blood if their lives depended on it. If once they had been God's warriors, they were now America's bankers. As far as she could tell, the only thing they were interested in was the stock market.

"Babe? You still up there?" Bryce called.

"Be down in a sec, sweetie," she called. The girlfriend role wasn't one she had played before, at least not for an assignment, although she had had boyfriends, of course— everyone did nowadays. It was becoming terribly fashionable to play with those eternal bonds, to flirt with destiny. The older generation was taken aback by how casual the newest incarnation of vampires were with their heavenly duties.

Look what had happened to Jack Force—a real shame. What a waste. He would be put on trial to burn the minute he returned to New York. If the Coven still existed, that is. Otherwise, Deming had no doubt that Mimi would hunt Jack down herself, even without a trial.

Deming was always careful not to get too involved with any boys, and to cut it off before it became serious. She knew as well as anyone that once you found your bondmate and identified each other in the cycle, it was Game Over.

As for Bryce, his immortal history had checked out clean as well, regardless of his dark angel profile. However, she noticed that his *affectus* was obscured, a cloudy white, which meant he was hiding something. Whether it had anything to do with Victoria's murder, Deming couldn't tell yet. She had to find a way to get closer to him somehow, so she could read his memory and find out what he was keeping in shadow. She didn't like to feel rushed, but with the Regent demanding daily reports, Deming had to find a way to ramp up her game.

The glom memory from Jamie Kip's apartment had backed up the eyewitness stories—Victoria had left Evan on the couch and hung out with Froggy and Bryce at the end of the party. There were no spirit traces that indicated an assault or a kidnapping in some way. If she had been taken against her will, Deming would have sensed it. No. Victoria had left with a friend, but one who was no friend to her. Was it Bryce? Was that what he was hiding? Had his dark angel tendencies taken over? She did not want to be prejudiced against him, but it was hard not to be when there was no other explanation.

Deming made sure the room was as messy as she'd found it and climbed down the stairs to find Bryce and his friends sprawled on the couches in the Kernochans' shrouded family room. Like many wealthy New Yorkers, their home was filled with museum-quality, priceless art and antiques lovingly chosen by a decorator on a monthly retainer. Yet, as Deming understood, no one ever used any of those beautiful, perfect rooms.

Instead, the designer always left one windowless room in the back, filled with comfortable couches and a giant TV, which meant that ninety percent of life in the town house was spent in one crowded room, while the rest of the expansive apartment sat empty, ready for its close-up for a *Shelter* magazine shoot that would never be allowed. The Blue Blood elite kept low profiles—the better to keep the masses from getting wind of their privilege and rising up to chop off their heads. Even if Marie Antoinette had survived (she was currently in cycle in the European Coven as one of the world's most famous and demanding movie stars—with her taste for cake intact), the vampires had learned their lesson.

"We were thinking of heading up to Rufus's in Greenwich. He's having people over this weekend," Bryce said. "Chopper's going to pick us up in an hour. We're staying over; you in?"

An overnight trip, twenty-four hours with her mysterious new boyfriend and her prime suspect in the death of an immortal. This was the opportunity she was looking for. She gave him a brilliant smile and promised to meet him at the helipad with her bags ready.

THIRTY-ONE

House Party

*T*he King estate sat on twenty acres of beachfront property in southwestern Connecticut. Rufus's father was one of those hedge fund types who had managed to make money off the recession instead of losing it, by betting *against* the economy. Deming wondered how much of that fit in with the Vampire Code to enlighten the human race. It seemed in the present, many of the vampires were not interested in helping humanity as much as they were interested in helping themselves to as much as possible.

It was dark when they arrived, the party already in full swing. Deming followed the boys into the house to find the hallway littered with tossed-off backpacks and discarded clothing. Loud rap music was playing, accompanied by splashing noises. Rufus King, who had graduated the year before and was a freshman at Yale, greeted them with expansive hugs. "Hey, thanks for coming. Pool's in the back."

The house had an outdoor pool covered by a tarp, as well as an indoor pool located in a glass atrium in the middle of the house. Deming walked with the group toward it. Bryce's friends were already in the water, so he immediately removed his pants, shirt, and socks and dove in with a loud whoop, wearing only his boxer shorts.

"Hey guys," she said, walking over to the clique of girls dangling their feet in the water.

"Oh hi, how was the copter ride?" Stella asked, but then turned away before Deming could answer. No one else bothered to say hello. Piper made a face before turning away. Piper had taken Deming's blow off the other day to heart, and had not been friendly ever since. But then again, Piper was exactly the sort of girl who would be annoyed that her new friend had found a boyfriend. Some girls were just built that way, and there was nothing Deming could do about it. Not that she cared. She wasn't here to make friends.

Deming felt a bit impatient for being stuck at a silly party. She was only there so she could finally cross Bryce Cutting off her suspect list. After tonight, if Bryce's *affectus* didn't reveal anything related to the case, she would take another look at the case file. She had been convinced that she would find her killer in this group of hedonistic self-centered teenagers, but after a week in their company, she began to think she might be on the wrong track. It annoyed her to have wasted so much time: Victoria's killer was still out there, and the Regent was counting on her to keep the Coven together.

She left the girls and found an empty bedroom, where she could change into her swimsuit. After she was dressed, she joined a bunch of kids who were gathered around the bar in the kitchen, surprised to find that a few of them were Red Bloods.

One of the boys looked up when she came near. "Hey, Deming, right?" he said. She had seen him around the Repository, arguing with another scribe who was stuffing books into boxes. The Regent was right to worry; the Conclave wasn't playing around. If Mimi couldn't find a way to stop them, they were going to take the vampires underground again.

"You're Oliver," she said, shaking his hand. "Mimi's friend." She had bumped into him once leaving the Regent's office.

Oliver's lips twitched. "That's a new one. She's not my friend here."

"Nor mine," she told him, and they shared a conspiratorial laugh.

"I didn't know there were going to be humans at the party," she told him, accepting a red Solo cup full of grain alcohol and a dash of Mountain Dew. The liquor was for the humans. It made their blood taste sweeter during the *Caerimonia*, for when the vampires would drink later.

"We're friends with Gemma Anderson, Stella's Conduit. As for all the one-lifers on the guest list, I think this is one of those recruitment parties," he said, meaning the Blue Bloods had invited a group of humans they thought would make good familiars. A "tasting party," they sometimes called it.

"Your hat's not in the ring, though," she said, noticing the small bite marks on his neck. "All the good ones are always taken."

Oliver smiled at that, but it was a wan smile, and it told her everything she had to know. Whoever his vampire was, she was no longer with him. Poor sap.

"Do you know Paul?" Oliver asked, turning to the guy hovering behind her.

"We're in Spirit of the Self together. Hi," Deming said.

"You mean Satan and Self-Interest," Paul said with a sly grin.

"The Devil will have his due," Oliver quipped. "I took that class last year. You guys are on *Paradise Lost* now?"

Deming took a sip from her cup and winced at the taste. "Yes, Paul here thinks Milton was too kind to Satan. Made him too much of a romantic figure for us to love."

"It's the bad-boy syndrome; chicks dig it," Paul said, his bright eyes flashing. "Speaking of," he mumbled under his breath, just as Deming felt a cold hand on her bare shoulder.

"There you are," Bryce said. He didn't bother to greet the other boys. "C'mon, we're out by the pool."

"Excuse me," Deming mouthed to Oliver and Paul as she walked away with Bryce. "God, you don't have to be so rude," she chided as they slipped into the shallow edge. "Just because they're Red Bloods, they're not completely useless.

One of them's in the Repository."

She wrapped her legs around Bryce under the water. "There's a room upstairs . . . just for us," she whispered, breathing into his ear. "You're not . . . bonded to anyone are you? Not yet, at least?"

"Nmm." He kissed her neck. "You?"

"Actually, I'm a starborn twin. I don't have a bondmate," she told him. It was a rare thing in the vampire world, to have a trueborn sibling. Starborn twins were two halves of the same person, made from the same empyrean star that split and produced two spirits instead of one and were identical in every aspect.

Deming would never understand the laws of the bloodbound, of the celestial soul mates. Of those who were self-contained and yet incomplete. Many of the starborn became Venators, like Sam and Ted Lennox.

Once every hundred years or so she had a romantic relationship with someone who had lost their bondmate, but mostly she kept to herself. Starborn vampires usually lived out their cycles alone.

But it didn't mean she had to be alone all the time.

"Meet me upstairs," she told Bryce. She was going to coax the dark angel out of his shadow.

Thirty-two

Interrogation

ryce loomed over her body, dark and gorgeous in the moonlight. She ran her fingers over his firm abdomen, tracing the line of each muscle. His kisses were deep and insistent, proving he was the kind of boy who always got what he wanted. Any other girl might have been thrilled, but after kissing for what seemed like hours, Deming was bored and impatient to get down to business.

He stopped kissing her neck for a moment and looked in her eyes. "Something wrong?" he asked huskily since she had stopped—what was she doing? Oh right, dutifully moaning and clutching his hair.

"No, not at all . . ." she said, and decided to go for it. It was one of the reasons she was such an effective Venator. She didn't need to use the glom to get people to tell the truth. She *seduced* it out of them. She became their best listener, a shoulder to cry on, someone to confess to, someone who understood. And now, with Bryce on top of her, it was the perfect time to ask something he did not expect to hear. "I'm worried about Victoria, what Stella said the other day. Do you think it's true? That maybe she's not in Switzerland and the Conclave is hiding something?"

"Who knows?" Bryce asked. "I mean, it's not the first time, right?"

"Did you know her well?"

"Vix? As well as anyone did," he said as he bent down to kiss the nape of her neck. She shivered a little from the draft coming in through the window, but Bryce took it as a response to his sensual ministrations and pressed down further. "I mean, she was a friend. Part of the group. You know," he murmured.

"Do you think anyone might have—I dunno—had something against her? Maybe that was why she had to go away?" she asked.

Bryce crushed his body against hers, but instead of responding in kind, Deming kept her body rigid. "Sometimes when kids have a hard time at school, their parents will send them somewhere else. Maybe Victoria was having a problem with someone—like Piper, maybe?"

He stopped his downward progression and wouldn't meet her eyes. She had chosen Piper's name at random and had not expected Bryce to react like he did. She felt his body turn cold all of a sudden. That was interesting.

"Piper didn't like her?" she asked.

"I didn't say that," he said, rolling off.

Now she knew there was *definitely* something here. His *affectus* was a deep shade of vermillion. She could see it all around his body, almost a physical reality. He was agitated, worried. He knew something about Piper and Victoria. Deming felt her heart rate quicken, but her face was a mask. Was she getting somewhere finally?

"Were they fighting? Did Victoria do something to Piper that might have made her mad?" she pressed.

"Not that I knew," Bryce said, scratching his nose. He seemed to shrink away, and his *affectus* began to pulse in shades of scarlet and black, shining like a flare in the darkness.

Deming charged into the glom, barreling through the wards that protected his spirit from intrusion. She pushed through the haze of his memory. Then she saw it: the memory that had triggered his agitation. The night of the party: Piper Crandall arguing with Victoria Taylor. She couldn't make out what the girls were saying—Bryce had been too far away to hear—but it was clear that Piper was extremely upset when they left together. Which meant that *Piper* was the last person who had seen Victoria alive. Victoria had left with Piper, and then Victoria was never seen again.

That was all she needed to see. Deming pulled away and scrambled into her clothes. She had to go over Piper's file again to see what she had missed.

"Where are you going?"

"I'm sorry, I forgot to tell you—I have to get back to the city tomorrow to meet my uncle," she said, without looking back.

She left Bryce alone in the bed and crept downstairs. It was past midnight and the party was over. Most of the Blue Bloods had left or retired to one of the numerous bedrooms. A few Red Bloods were slumped on the couch or passed out on the floor, abandoned by their new masters.

"Hey!" she said, coming across Paul Rayburn as he walked out the front door. "Devil boy."

"Oh, hey, what's up," he said, looking surprised to see her. She noticed his neck had no bite marks, which meant he had not been chosen. He was cute enough, but Deming figured most of the vamp chicks at the party didn't go for the smart and sensitive type. "Thin-blooded," they called it. She felt an odd sense of relief at that, which puzzled her. Why would she care if another vampire had marked him as her own?

"Are you taking off?" she asked. She had planned to run all the way back, at *Velox* speed, but the journey would tire her. "Are you going into Manhattan? Can you give me a ride?"

"Actually . . ." He looked around. "I was waiting for someone. But it's all right. Yeah, sure. Why not. I've got my brother's car."

"Great." She smiled. "I'm in the Village."

THIRTY-THREE

A Tale of Two Friends

*P*aul Rayburn drove with his hands on the wheel at two and ten o'clock. He kept glancing at Deming shyly. He cleared his throat. "I thought you were with Bryce."

"I was," Deming yawned. "But not anymore." That was definitely done. She had no more use for Bryce Cutting now that she knew his secret.

"That was quick. . . . What are you, some kind of heartbreaker?" Paul asked.

"Since when are you so concerned with my love life?" she teased.

Paul looked over his shoulder to change lanes, and their eyes met briefly. "Since the beginning."

He had a crush on her. She had thought as much, had read it in his *affectus* every time he looked at her. Deming felt an odd thrill. She'd left a dark angel panting in a bedroom upstairs, but in a car with a mere mortal she found she was feeling something she hadn't felt just few minutes ago. *Interest. Attraction.* It turned out, smart and sensitive was *her* type. She began to wonder what his blood tasted like—she bet those prejudices were wrong.

"I have to warn you, though, you're not going to get rid of me as easily as that," Paul said.

"No?"

"No, I mean—if you were my girlfriend, I'd make sure, for instance, that you didn't leave a party with some other dude."

"What else would you do?" she asked, curious.

"I'm not going to tell you." He blushed.

"Because I can imagine quite a lot." She smiled. This was fun. The conventional wisdom on why certain humans were chosen as familiars was that it was a purely physical response on the vampire's part, submitting to the allure of the blood chemistry. Deming had yet to mark a human as her familiar. While more and more vampires were taking their familiars at a younger age, she didn't plan on doing so until her eighteenth birthday.

When Paul reached over to remove the iPod in the glove compartment, his hand accidentally brushed hers, and Deming felt an electric jolt of energy pass between them. It was as if she was a match that had lit with his touch. Suddenly, she couldn't breathe. Was this what everyone was talking about? Was this the bloodlust? Until now, she had never experienced it—the hunger, the acute, unmistakable desire for a certain human being's blood. It was as if her entire body were calling for a taste of his blood, and she would not be satisfied until she drank from him.

"You all right? You look a little pale."

"I'm okay." Deming looked away. She put a hand up to cover her mouth. Her fangs were protruding; her mouth was *watering*. She wanted him. She wanted him so badly it took all of her concentration to stop herself from jumping him. Whatever this was, she had no time for it. Even if she wanted Paul and was experiencing bloodlust for the first time, she had to focus. She had a job to do.

"How'd you know those guys?" she asked, affecting a casual air, and trying not to notice the electricity buzzing between them. "Through Gemma?"

"Uh-huh. But Piper invited me. She kind of had to since I was standing next to her at the time. It was a pity invite."

At the mention of Piper's name, Deming refocused her energy. "Piper's nice. . . ." she said, letting him take the lead. She wanted to find out what other people thought about Piper. Bryce's memory was one piece of the puzzle, but if she was going to pin this on Piper Crandall she'd need a lot more information to build her case.

Paul changed lanes again. "Piper's all right. You guys hang out, huh?"

"Kind of. I heard she was pretty tight with some girl named Victoria Taylor, who left before I got here."

He fiddled with the stereo and the car swerved a little.

"Oh great, I missed my exit. Sorry, what were you saying? Piper and Victoria?" he asked, as the Cowboy Junkies played in the background.

"They were best friends?" Deming prompted.

"You mean they were friends, until . . ."

"Until?" Deming leaned closer.

Paul glanced at her. "Look, I don't listen to gossip, especially about those who are basically unaware of my existence; it's too demeaning. But what can I say? I go to this school, I'm not deaf. I heard that Victoria and Bryce were hooking up and Piper found out the night of Jamie Kip's party."

"Really? Victoria and Bryce? They were together?" She hadn't found any indication of that in the reports, and Victoria had not played a prominent role in any of Bryce's memories.

"Yeah. And it really pissed Piper off." It was clear that Paul was lying when he said he did not enjoy gossip. He was bathed in a yellow light, warm and glowing, illuminating his features.

"But why would Piper care?"

"Piper and Bryce used to date." Paul shrugged. "I thought everyone knew that."

So that's what the girls had been arguing about at the party, why Piper had looked so murderous. This was the secret rancor Deming had been searching for, the poison inside the apple. She understood the dark violent emotions that claimed lives and caused people to burn and torture their best friends, to decide that they were no better than a pile of wood chips. As a Venator she had seen the consequences that the bitterness of resentment and jealousy could bring to a seemingly close friendship. Piper and Victoria had loved the same dark angel.

Piper and Bryce had been together, but Victoria had come between them. Jealousy over a boy had turned one friend against the other. Deming didn't think Bryce knew what Piper had done, but he had suspected enough to feel guilty about it. The night of Jamie Kip's party, Piper discovered that her best friend had betrayed her.

Finally, Deming had what she was looking for: a motive.

THIRTY-FOUR

Bond Less

*P*iper Crandall glared at her from across the interrogation table. The Lennox brothers had picked the suspect up Monday afternoon from school, and had taken her to Venator headquarters for questioning.

"You!" she spat, the minute she saw Deming enter the windowless room. "What do you want? What's this all about? They said I had to come down to answer some questions. You're a freaking Venator? What is this?"

"I want to talk about Victoria Taylor," Deming replied coolly. She had ditched the fashion plate schoolgirl attire and was dressed in regulation Venator black. For the first time since arriving in New York, Deming felt like herself again. It was a relief to stop wearing the disguise. She'd spent the weekend pulling files and putting her case together. She was ready.

"What about Victoria?" Piper asked nervously.

Deming turned to the television screen on the wall, and hit PLAY. "Have you seen this video?" she asked.

"Sure, it's all over the Internet. Some kind of vampire movie from the Conspiracy."

"It's not a movie trailer. It's real. And that's Victoria in the video. Here's another. Look familiar?" Deming played the video of Victoria's burning and tried not to flinch, but it was hard to watch.

The color drained from Piper's face, and she pressed her hands to her eyes. "Oh my God. Oh my God. Is she—oh my God—is that really . . . no . . . no. No, Victoria, no. She's supposed to be at Le Rosey . . . what happened . . . oh my God . . ."

Deming cut her off. The girl was a good actress, she had to hand it to her, but she wasn't buying one second of it. "The night of Jamie Kip's party, you found out that your best friend was dating your ex-boyfriend."

"What are you talking about?" Piper sobbed, her eyes and nose bright red. "Victoria is dead? Oh my God. What happened? Who did this to her?"

Deming felt a moment of pity, but she had seen this all before—suspects who could not admit to the horror of their crime, who honestly believed in their hearts that they had never harmed their loved ones. She continued her relentless interrogation. "Victoria came between the two of you, and you wanted to punish her. You wanted her dead, and you covered it up with a conspiracy threat to disguise the real reason. To hide your motive."

When she had gone over Piper's file again, Deming noticed that Piper was a junior member of the Conspiracy. As such, she had insider knowledge on the workings of the subcommittee; she knew which buttons to push and how to create the illusion of a real security breach.

"I don't understand," Piper whimpered. "Victoria . . . why . . . oh God, why . . . ?"

"Why is right. Why did you want her dead? Because she came between the most sacred relationship you had in the world. Because you and Bryce Cutting are *bondmates*."

When it came down to it, everything always went back to the bond. Being bondless herself, Deming could never quite understand what the fuss was about. From what she could see, the bond just made everything more complicated.

This was just like the kidnapping in Shanghai, where instead of exposure, money was used as a smoke screen. The vampire who had taken Liling was convinced he was her bondmate, and wanted to hurt her for falling in love with someone else. He'd meant to take the Code into his own hands. Deming had saved the girl just in time. Good thing too, since in the end, the boy had been mistaken. There was no bond between them and there never had been.

Some vampires thought the bond was all about love stories and romance. Souls calling out to each other through the centuries. But Deming knew nothing was ever that simple. Not in the matters of the heart and the bond. Victoria

Taylor wasn't the first to suffer because of a bond, and she would not be the last.

After the shattering silence, Piper finally spoke. "Took you long enough to figure that out, huh?" she said bitterly, wiping away her tears. "That Bryce was mine. You sure didn't care about that when you were hooking up with him at Rufus's party."

Deming blushed. "That isn't important."

"No? Well how about this, Venator? I don't know where you got the stupid idea that Victoria 'stole' Bryce from me, and I killed her. You're absolutely wrong on that count. Victoria was my friend. She was the best friend I ever had. She never came between us. Ask anyone in school. Victoria didn't even *like* Bryce. She couldn't believe he was my vampire twin. 'Not that douche,' were her words. Yeah, it pissed me off. But it pissed me off more that the night of Jamie's party, Bryce wouldn't acknowledge that we had found each other. He wanted more space, he said. He wanted more time, to be *sure*. I was so angry at him, and Vix was trying to calm me down, so I lashed out at her. But Vix was a real friend. In fact, no one has ever come between Bryce and me but *you*, you bondless freak. Get me a blood trial. Scan my freaking subconscious. I'm telling the truth."

THIRTY-FIVE

The Second Victim

*D*eming was shaking when she left the interrogation room. Ted Lennox looked at her with sympathy. "It's clear as day in the glom."

"I know." She collapsed on the nearest chair. She'd seen it too, more clearly than they, who'd needed to be in the twilight world to see Piper's *affectus*.

She had been so sure—Victoria going after Bryce explained everything—nothing was more anathema in the Blue Blood community than someone who came between the bond. Nothing. Just look at the Force twins.

When she'd asked him about Piper, Bryce Cutting had looked guilty and felt guilty and was guilty because he *knew* he was cheating on his bondmate. Bringing up Piper's name while he was hooking up with Deming had spooked him. Bryce had reacted to *Piper*'s name, sure, but not for the reason Deming had believed.

Deming had been so certain of her talent for reading the *affectus*, she had immediately jumped to the conclusion that Piper was the murderer, that the threat of losing the bond had driven her to hatch an elaborate plot that entailed the murder of her best friend. She couldn't have been more wrong if she'd tried.

Sam Lennox popped out of the glom and gripped her shoulder. "Sorry. It was a good guess, though."

A good guess but not good enough. Not the truth. She was back to the beginning. Back where she had started. In the dark. Nowhere. The Lennox brothers were being kind, but their disappointment said it all.

"By the way, as soon as you can, the Regent wants to see you in her office," Sam said quietly.

When she arrived at headquarters, Deming was ushered into a small waiting room. She was made to wait for a few hours, with nothing but the drone of FNN on the television screen and old magazines to keep her company. Finally Mimi's secretary arrived. "She's ready for you now, dear," Doris said.

Deming entered the office and took a seat across from the massive desk. The Regent was certainly in a foul mood. The Venator thought she had never seen a person with a blacker *affectus*, and steeled herself for a tongue-lashing.

But after a heavy silence, Mimi only sighed. "You're very lucky. Piper's so traumatized from learning about

Victoria's death that the Crandalls have decided not to file a complaint."

"I assume complete responsibility. If you'd like me to resign . . ." Deming said, looking squarely at her superior with her head held high. What happened that morning was a blow to her ego, but she had no time for self-pity. She felt a huge amount of shame, and promised herself she would make it up to Piper by bringing Victoria's real murderer to justice.

"No. I don't accept. We need you more than ever. While you were breaking down your suspect, this arrived in my in-box." Mimi flipped her screen around so Deming could watch. This time, the video was much shorter. It was just a freeze frame of a bound and shackled vampire. But the message was the same. *On the eve of the crescent moon, watch the vampire burn.*

"Who is it?" Deming asked, stoic in the face of this new disaster.

"Stuart Rhodes. Duchesne senior. He's been missing since Rufus King's party in Connecticut. Saturday night. You were there, weren't you?"

"Yes." Deming reviewed her memories from that evening, but she had been so busy with Bryce she hadn't paid attention to anyone else, hadn't noticed anything odd. Stuart Rhodes. Who was Stuart Rhodes? He wasn't part of the in-crowd. But it had been a tasting party, which meant every Blue Blood at Duchesne was usually invited. Deming had a vague memory of a small, quiet boy standing to the side, watching everyone from behind glass-bottom lenses.

"Anyway, it's the same thing. Just like Victoria's video," Mimi said.

"Is there any link between Victoria Taylor and Stuart Rhodes?"

"As far I know, none. Stuart is not . . . Well, let's just say he had his own friends," Mimi said delicately.

"You think this is random, then?"

The Regent shrugged. "Isn't that for you to find out? Anyway, just like before, his location has been masked. We can't find him in the glom."

"This thing's on the Internet?" she asked, motioning to the screen.

Mimi nodded. "Yes, but the Conspiracy's working to add the *Suck* movie tagline on it. That should be up within an hour."

"Good, that takes care of exposure."

"But it doesn't help us find our victim," Mimi pointed out. "You heard the video, and this time we only have three days until the next crescent moon. I've managed to keep the Conclave unaware of this new hostage for now. I can't take the wards down again; not that it helped us any last time. So start doing what I brought you here to do. You'd better come up with something, Chen! Find me my killer! Find Stuart! Or I swear to God when the Coven dies, I'll take you down with me." The Regent did not need the help of the glom to look like a wrathful Angel of Death just then.

But Deming remained unperturbed in her seat. "Understood."

"You seem awfully confident," Mimi huffed. "What are you planning?"

"What I should've done the minute I arrived in New York. A DeathWalk."

THIRTY-SIX

Background Checks

The next morning the Lennox brothers listened intently as Deming outlined what they would need to help her prepare for the mission. After yesterday's humiliation she had believed she would never be able to work in New York again, that her fellow Venators would demand she be taken off the case and shipped back directly to China. Instead the brothers were being extraordinarily understanding. It happened all the time, they assured her. Venator work was not infallible. They made mistakes. What was important was that they kept trying.

The plan was for the three of them to enter the glom together, with Sam keeping an eye out for danger and staying at the top level, while Ted would follow her as far as he could into the spirit trail, stopping just below the subconscious layer. Once Deming flatlined she would be able to go underneath the masking spell, locate Stuart, and pull his body out of the real world and into the glom, where the boys would be waiting to help, and then the four of them would jump out together.

"Still sounds risky," Sam said, shaking his head. "Once you're in the protoconscious, you're on your own, and you might not be able to get back into your body in time."

"Yes, technically I'll be dead for five minutes and my heart will stop beating. But five minutes out here is like five hours in the glom. I'll have plenty of time."

"It's your call."

Deming nodded. "We'll do it tomorrow night. I need a day to get ready."

To prepare for a DeathWalk she had to familiarize herself with every aspect of her victims' current and past incarnations. Given the immortal history of the Blue Bloods, one could never predict what one might find in a Death-Walk, and it was best to be prepared. She had a hunch Stuart Rhodes was not a random victim even though he had no apparent link to Victoria Taylor. From her innumerable cycles as a Truth Seeker, Deming knew that things were rarely as they seemed, and while it might appear on the surface that Victoria Taylor and Stuart Rhodes had no connection to each other, the reality was usually a lot more complicated.

Stuart Rhodes's cycle mother was out of the county, and Deming left a message with her assistant to call her back as soon as Mrs. Rhodes was able. In the meantime, Victoria

Taylor's cycle mother agreed to meet Deming for a cup of coffee that afternoon. Even if there was nothing more she could do for Victoria, Deming thought maybe the cycle parents would know something that might help her current case, to see if there was any connection between the two victims.

She met Gertrude Taylor at the MOMA café that afternoon. Gertrude was one of the museum's premier trustees, a hard-working Committee member. The Taylors had been told of Victoria's demise but had been denied the ability to grieve, as the Regent had insisted on keeping everything classified until the case was solved. According to the Venator reports, the Taylors were hands-off parents who barely knew their daughter, so Deming did not know what to expect.

"How lovely to meet you." Gertrude smiled and took a seat at the bustling café.

"Thanks for meeting me, Mrs. Taylor."

"Oh, it's Gertrude, and I know you're not a student at Duchesne, really. You're the Venator they brought in to find out who did this to Victoria, yes?"

"I aim to." Deming nodded.

"Good." Gertrude stirred her green tea. Up close, Deming could see the deep lines around her eyes. While the woman gave every outward indication of serenity and contentment, her face bore a shadow of sorrows that no amount of plastic surgery or vampire genes could mask. The reports were wrong. This woman was clearly suffering. "Victoria was our first. We've never been asked to carry a spirit before. Our names came up in the House of Records and we were thrilled. Victoria was the most sweet-tempered child. She always had so many friends. I can't imagine how anyone would want to harm her, especially someone who knew her."

"What about an earlier cycle? Was there anything in her past that might indicate . . . a grudge? A weakness? Anything?"

"I don't recall."

Deming took out her notepad. "When was her last incarnation? Did she tell you?"

"Let me see. I think when the Transformation began and Victoria started having the blood memories, she said she believed she was last in cycle in Florence, around the fifteenth century or so—she remembered being in Michelangelo's studio. The House of Records would have her file, I should think. Sometimes the blood memory isn't so reliable at her age."

"Thanks very much, you've been really helpful."

"No, thank you. The Conclave has kept us in the dark about all this, but we're very glad to hear they've put someone of your caliber in charge." Gertrude Taylor rose from the table and shook Deming's hand, her eyes bright with tears. For a moment she did not look like an intimidating society matron or a fallen angel, merely a mother mourning her daughter.

* * *

A few hours later, Stuart Rhodes's mother finally returned Deming's call. The Rhodeses were anthropologists, and currently in Egypt for a dig. From reading Stuart's file, Deming observed that he had practically raised himself. Once the Transformation set in, he was barely supervised.

Amelia Rhodes did not seem particularly distraught over her son's disappearance. "Sounds as if it's just some kind of prank, doesn't it?" she asked over the roar of helicopters. "I spoke to Stuart just a few days ago. He was going to some party and was pretty excited about it. He doesn't get invited out much, you know."

"I'm afraid it's not a prank, ma'am. The Regent has given me permission to inform you that what has happened to Stuart happened to another student at Duchesne, another vampire in our community." Deming filled her in on the gory details. "Stuart is in grave danger."

"Well, what do you want us to do? We didn't ask for this."

"You didn't petition the House of Records for a cycle birthing?" Deming asked.

"A long time ago. In my past life I thought I should try to experience being a mother. By the time they got around to my number, I was bored of the idea."

"If there's anything you can tell us about him, it would be helpful in saving his life. Do you remember if he was beginning to have any indication of his past incarnations? Of when he was in cycle last?"

"He did mention it, but I can't remember. Somewhere in Europe, maybe? I'm sorry. You will find him, won't you? Before they burn him like they did this poor girl? I have become quite fond of the boy. With our work, his father and I don't get to see him that often, but we do miss him."

THIRTY-SEVEN

The House of Records

*T*hat night Deming studied her case files again, paying close attention to the notes on the obscure message the Venators had found in the original video. She had dismissed it as a mere distraction at first but now she took a second look. The head of the Repository believed they had cracked the code and that the three images—Lucifer's sigil, the sheep, which stood for humanity, and the symbol for union—indicated that the Morningstar was in league with Red Bloods. If so, it meant that whoever had made the video and had taken the hostages was part of this movement. A human in service to Croatan? It was simply unheard of, which was why she had ignored it as a diversion. To think that it might be real unsettled the usually stoic Venator.

Before sunrise, she crept into Duchesne to pick up her

lucky jade turtle from her locker—it was a silly superstition but she didn't want to do a DeathWalk without it. Her twin had bought them the tiny figurines in a Hong Kong market, and Deming had made it a habit to bring the little guy wherever she went. She wanted to slip in and out without anyone noticing or asking any questions. With the early hour, the school was empty save for the janitors, so she was surprised to bump into Paul Rayburn walking out of the third-floor library with a cart of books. The junior lockers were located right across from the library doors.

"Paul, hey," she said.

"Oh hey," he said, his *affectus* turning the usual shade of orange in her presence.

"What are you doing here?"

"I'm a library aide. Part of the work study program," Paul said, jangling keys. "I try to get my work done before school. It's better than staying late." He looked sleepy and tired, and Deming was moved by how much effort being a student at Duchesne must have cost him. It couldn't be easy to be poor around such wealth.

She felt the now-familiar stirrings of bloodlust in his presence, but his shy smile invoked a different reaction as well, one that went deeper than the impulse to drink his blood. "It's not even morning yet," she said as she stuffed her files into her book bag. She realized that her heart hurt a little, knowing that after today she would probably never see him again. Once she found Stuart, and she was certain she would, her assignment would be complete and she would leave the country.

It was a pity, since she felt something for Paul, a queasy mixture of desire and affection that she could not figure out. And it scared her because her life until now had been about order and discipline. Her feelings for him were a distraction. They would only cloud her judgment, if they hadn't already. The best Venators were unencumbered by emotion, and Deming strove to be the best.

"Yeah, well." He shrugged. "I'm used to it. What brings you here so early?"

"Honestly, I couldn't sleep," she told him.

"Maybe we can catch up later? When we're both awake?"

She was about to shake her head when it occurred to her that maybe instead of running away from her feelings she should see where this was going so she could completely shut it down. "I'd like that. How about this time tomorrow? A sunrise breakfast?"

Paul gave her a dazzling smile that made Deming momentarily forget she had asked him to meet her only so she could crush any romantic ideas he might harbor about the two of them.

Only when he left did she realize she had forgotten to ask him about what he'd told her about Victoria, Bryce, and Piper. She wanted to know where he had heard that piece of false information.

* * *

The House of Records was located in the midtown headquarters, in a restricted section of the Repository. The clerk stared balefully at the black-clad Venator as he handed over a yellowing stack of paper. "Regent sign the warrant?"

"I have it right here," Deming said, handing over the certificate with Mimi's flowery signature. The Regent had agreed to open the file just for this instance.

"Privileged information, this is. Not just anything everyone should know," the walleyed clerk grumbled.

"I understand that. That's why I have a warrant," Deming said patiently.

"Take the fourth cubicle."

"Thank you."

Deming settled into her desk and began to page through the cycle birth records for Victoria Taylor and Stuart Rhodes. Looking into an immortal's past cycles was verboten in the Coven. The Code of the Vampires decreed that each vampire come into the knowledge of past lifetimes on their own, through the Blood Manifest—not through looking up files and records in a library. Lawrence Van Alen had been instrumental in preaching that identities came from within—that even if you had lived an immortal life, recorded diligently by scribes since the dawn of time, it was still your duty to discover your destiny on your own rather than have your past handed to you on typewritten sheets.

STUART RHODES
Birth Name: Hollis Stuart Cobden Rhodes
Known Past Lives: Piero d'Argento (Florence)

VICTORIA TAYLOR
Birth Name: Victoria Alexandra Forbes Taylor
Known Past Lives: Stefana Granacci (Florence)

That was interesting. Both Victoria Taylor and Stuart Rhodes were last in cycle in the same place and during the same time period. So even if they did not know each other in the present, there was a distinct possibility they had known each other in the past. It couldn't be a coincidence.

In any event, once she was in the glom she would find Stuart, apprehend his abductors, and she would finally have her answers.

Deming left the Repository, her head bowed low. The Lennox boys were meeting her back at Venator headquarters in an hour, and she would have a little time to get herself ready before they arrived. She went through a checklist in her head; she would have to remember to wear something warm. The last time she had woken up from the procedure, she had been shaking with cold.

She would call her twin. She wanted to hear Dehua's voice, and not just in the glom. Just another superstition, like the green turtle she held in her hand. Other than that, there was nothing else; she was ready to walk into the valley of the shadow.

As she waited for the light to change, she recognized a car parked across the street. It was the same one that had taken her home Saturday evening. Paul was at the wheel. She was about to wave to him when she saw he wasn't alone. There was a girl with him.

There was something familiar about the girl getting out of the car.

Then Deming realized.

She was Victoria Taylor.

THIRTY-EIGHT

Confessions

For a moment Deming was too stunned to move, but recovered quickly so that in a flash she was not only in Paul's car, she had a hand on the wheel. "Pull over," she demanded.

Paul jumped. He looked terrified to see her appear out of nowhere. "How did you—?" he asked, barely missing hitting a speeding taxicab. Deming turned the wheel toward the curb, and the car came to a crashing stop.

"That girl you were with. Who was she?" Deming did not have time for any more lies and nonsense. She wanted to get to the bottom of this. Now. She'd had a choice between following the girl and confronting Paul, and she chose to hear the truth from him.

"What girl?"

"The girl who got out of your car back there. Victoria Taylor." It was Victoria, she was sure. Deming had studied her photograph numerous times and had memorized the girl's face. She would know Victoria anywhere.

Paul scoffed. "Victoria? Isn't she in like, Switzerland or something?"

"You're lying. You've been lying since the beginning," she said softly. She didn't need to interrogate him to know. "That whole thing with Piper and Bryce and Victoria was a huge lie."

Paul slumped against the wheel. "Okay, fine, I lied about that. But if you want me to tell the truth, you'll have to do the same."

Deming raised a quizzical eyebrow. "I don't follow."

"I know what you are. You don't have to keep your secret from me. I know you're one of them."

"One of who?"

He looked into her eyes. "I know the Committee's just a cover. That there are people in this world who don't die, who keep coming back every hundred years."

"You're insane. I have no idea what you are talking about." My God, had they been this sloppy? How was it that he knew their secrets? Talk about a security breach. Paul was neither a Conduit nor a familiar. How did he know?

Paul cleared his throat and looked out the window, and answered as if he had heard her question. "I've been a student at Duchesne for a couple of years now. I've seen things. I've heard things. Guys like Bryce Cutting are pretty careless. I know most of the kids at school are blind, but I'm not.

I know what you are. And it's okay."

Deming shook her head. "I don't know what you're talking about," she said evenly. "What I do want to talk about is why Victoria Taylor was in your car just now."

"It's a stalemate then," Paul said amiably. "You want me to tell you the truth, but then you won't give me the courtesy of doing the same."

Suddenly, Deming remembered the words from the video. *Vampires are real. Open your eyes. They are all around us. Do not believe the lies they tell.*

Then Paul's words: *People who don't know I exist. It's demeaning.* She had dismissed his attitude as the usual resentment against the popular crowd, but it was more than that. He had a key to the school, and Victoria had been hidden in the attic. Then with a start she realized two things had been bothering since she'd learned of Stuart Rhodes's kidnapping. One, that at Rufus's party, Stuart had been standing next to Paul Rayburn. They were friends. Two, that it was a tasting party. The only humans invited were familiars and those who were about to become familiars. And yet Paul Rayburn had left the party unchosen. No bite marks. That was not supposed to happen. Committee rules forbade such a thing. Paul had seen too much—he should have been marked.

Deming had another epiphany. Jamie Kip's party was closed as well—only vampires and Conduits, familiars or about-to-be-familiars. Evan Howe had entered the party an ordinary boy and had left as Victoria Taylor's familiar. Deming would bet that Paul Rayburn had been at Jamie Kip's party—who knows how many parties—and had left unchanged. Unclaimed. Here was a human who did not feel any loyalty to the vampires, and yet was privy to their secrets.

Then she saw it as she looked into his bright blue eyes— the memory that had eluded her so far. The night of Jamie's party, Victoria was arguing with Piper, and had stormed off. She had made it as far as the hallway, when Paul had come out of the shadows and placed a black bag over her head and dragged her back inside. He had waited until the changing of the Wardens at dawn to slip away with his hostage. That way no one had seen them. No records. No eyewitnesses.

Deming felt a sense of horror at her discovery. Paul meant something to her. When she'd bumped into him that morning she knew it was more than just bloodlust. She'd felt something for him she hadn't before, in centuries of being alive. Attraction. Affection. Respect. Admiration. Love? Maybe. It could have been. But now they would never know.

"Why, Paul?" Deming asked.

He smiled. "I'd suspected there was something going on for a long time, but I wanted to know for sure. Especially when my pal Stuart was tapped to be part of this 'Committee' and I wasn't. It didn't make sense that he would get in and I wouldn't. So one afternoon I hid in the library during one of their meetings and I saw and heard everything. I confronted Stuart—told him I knew, that I shot some video too, and I was going to put it up on the Internet, show everyone the truth.

"The whole world should know what you guys are. You run the place and no one even *knows*. It's not fair. You're not gods."

"No, we aren't," Deming agreed softly, thinking of that ancient battle in Heaven. "We aren't gods." They had certainly learned that the hard way.

"Why are you looking at me that way? You think I did something wrong? No way. It was all Victoria's idea to play hostage. Do you even think a human could overcome a vampire? Be serious. Anyway, I told Stuart what I was going to do, and he told her. She came to me and asked me not to post the video yet. She had something better in mind. She said that she and Stuart were in love, and they wanted to leave the Coven because they weren't allowed to be together.

"They were 'bonded' to other people. But if these other people found out, Stuart and Victoria would burn. They were scared of the—what do you guys call her—the Regent? They talked about Jack Force—about how what was planned for him would happen to them if anyone found out. So Victoria came up with this hostage thing. She said if we could make it seem like they'd died, no one would ever come looking for them. She said she knew how to fool even the Venators.

"She gave me detailed instructions. She was really

concerned about timing. She said they were being watched all the time."

Deming nodded. How would Paul have known about the Wardens otherwise? She hadn't paid much attention to his *affectus* before, when he'd told her that fanciful tale about Victoria and Piper, but she was paying attention now. Everything she was reading indicated that he was telling the truth.

"I know you don't have any reason to believe me. I heard about you. Stuart told me. His dad is on the Conclave. You're some kind of super-vampire sleuth or something."

"What else did Stuart tell you?"

"That Victoria's waiting for him. See, she's been in the city the entire time. They're leaving for the European Coven. By tomorrow everyone would believe Stuart was dead, and they were free to go."

So if everything he was telling her was true, and his *affectus* seemed to prove it, plus the fact that Victoria, a vampire, could never have been subdued by a human against her will, then it was all a prank—a silly prank made by vampires who were in love with the wrong people and wanted to leave the Coven, and a human boy who wanted in on a big secret. Maybe the biggest secret of all.

"Listen, I know what you're thinking: you want to wipe my memory or something, right? Stuart and Victoria wanted to as well, but I managed to talk them out of it. Please don't."

Deming fiddled with the chopsticks in her hair. "No, a

memory wipe won't take care of it. You know too much. If I did it, you could have . . . brain damage."

Paul glanced at the locked car door. "Then you're going to do the other thing. But maybe there's another way. I don't want that. Maybe I can be one of those human . . . what do you call it . . . Conduits or something."

"Conduits are born, not made. It's not an open position. The Coven would never allow it. I'm sorry. There's only one way." She knew what she had to do. Something that should have been done by someone a long time ago. Maybe that's why she had been so attracted to him, because she knew in the end, she would have to do this.

"Don't," Paul said, holding her hand. "Don't make me lesser than you. Treat me as an equal, as you have been. I'm just human, but it's our blood that keeps you alive. Without us, you are nothing."

He put a soft hand to her cheek. "Meet me on my own terms. Share yourself with me as a *person*. I know about the Sacred Kiss. I know what it does. What it will do to me."

His *affectus* pulsated with the blue of the open sea and of the endless sky. Blue was the color of truth. He loved her. That was why she'd felt her stomach churn when she'd seen Victoria Taylor in his car. She had trusted him and he had lied to her. But he had only lied to protect his friends. He was so heartbreakingly lovely, she could weep. Deming touched his neck and whispered, "I love you too."

THIRTY-NINE

Puppetmaster

*J*ust as Paul had said, it was all a big fake. That evening the Venator team swarmed his small bedroom. Sam was searching the glom memory while Ted and a tech aide worked on the computer.

"Take a look," Ted called, pointing to the screen.

Deming leaned over and read the e-mail. It was from Victoria Taylor.

Paul, Thank you for everything. The European Coven has agreed to take us. I cannot wait until Stuart and I are together again. You are a true friend. —Victoria

Everything had been staged as meticulously as a small theatrical production. Victoria had procured a corpse from the morgue. That was the body of the girl who had burned in Newport. There were dozens and dozens of e-mails from Stuart and Victoria. They had planned to leave the country the day of Stuart's alleged burning. The whole thing was a hoax, an escape plan hidden within a conspiracy threat.

Luckily, it had all worked out for the best. No vampires had been harmed. Everyone thought *Suck* was a movie. The Red Bloods were still in the dark.

"You guys picking up Victoria and Stuart?" Deming asked.

"According to this they're meeting at JFK in an hour. We'll be there," replied Ted.

"The attic?"

"Checked out. His fingerprints were all over the computer, and fibers from the trunk of the car matched Stuart's DNA."

Deming realized Stuart had likely been in the trunk the night they had left Rufus King's party. So that was why Paul had looked so nervous when she'd asked him for a ride.

Sam Lennox returned from the glom. "Nothing here but boredom and loneliness," he said. "No sign of any violence or agitation. Looks like the kid was telling the truth."

It was just as she'd thought. Deming nibbled on her cuticles. Unlike the pretty story Paul had told her about Piper, in this one, everything had been as he'd described.

Deming felt relieved. She had gotten to the truth this time. Or had she? A nagging doubt remained. Everything fit too well, too simply . . . whether it was because it was the truth or because Paul had prepared another elaborate lie, she just wasn't sure. She had to cover all her bases.

"It's too easy," she muttered.

"What are you thinking?" Sam asked.

"Look, you guys kept those ashes from that burning, right? Have the bloodline checked. Just confirm that it wasn't Victoria."

"Done." Ted nodded and called into the Venator team back at the Repository to order the test.

"Keep a team on Rayburn," Deming ordered. "He'll be waking up soon enough. Then when you guys are done here, meet me back at Bleecker. I want to take another look at those masking spells. Make sure everything checks out."

FORTY

DeathWalk

hen the Lennox brothers met Deming back at Venator quarters, one look at their drawn faces told her all she had to know. Sam sunk into the nearest battered armchair. "You were right. The bloodline is unmistakable. Victoria Taylor is dead. She's been dead for weeks."

"And we checked the bond records," Ted added. "Victoria didn't have a bondmate in this cycle. Stuart didn't either. They were free agents. At least in this lifetime. But in any event, they weren't together, and they never were. It was all a lie. All the e-mails were faked."

Deming kept her calm, but her hands were shaking. "Stuart Rhodes?"

Sam shook his head. "The only thing we found at the airport terminal was an urn with remains. The lab's going through it now, but I have a hunch it's Stuart. Looks like the body's been dead for three days. The video was a lie. There was no saving him from the beginning."

"Where's Paul?" she asked.

If it were possible to look more desolate, Ted Lennox managed it. "The team lost him a few hours ago. He slipped away; they don't know how. Look, whoever or whatever this guy is, he's dangerous. He's not one of us, and he's killed two vampires already. He's able to conjure a doppelgänger. That's real dark magic right there." The Venators had found no trace of the girl in Paul's car in the glom memory, which meant she had never existed.

"And according to you he's able to manipulate his *affectus*. You'd better be careful down there," Sam warned. "Are you sure we can't talk you out of this?"

"No. I need to do this," Deming said. What had Paul said to her? *I heard about you, that you were coming.* He had been able to prepare. He knew all about her. He knew that she relied on her talent, her facile way of knowing what was so hard for other Venators to read. He knew she would be proud of it, arrogant even. He had found a way to use her talent against her.

But he hadn't counted on her ability to learn from her mistakes. She might have been fooled once, but he was wrong to think she would fall for a love story again.

"Right. But even if we can't find him on this side, we'll find him in the glom. I'm going in. We have a DeathWalk to complete."

* * *

Every vampire experienced the glom in a different way. For Deming, the twilight world manifested as an empty plaza in the middle of the Forbidden City, in Beijing. It had been years since she had seen the Forbidden City this way in real life. Nowadays it was crowded with so many tourists it was hard to comprehend the magnitude of its beauty. But in the glom, the ancient walled city was silent and empty.

She walked past the guardhouse, through the Outer Court to the Inner one, taking the Imperial Way, a path that was only reserved for the Emperor, until she was standing in the steps of the Hall of Mental Cultivation, which meant she was deep in the protoconscious. In the physical world, her heart stopped beating. She walked the line between the worlds, in the thin membrane that separated the living and the dead.

Paul was waiting for her at the steps of the farthest pavilion. In the glom, his soul was even more beautiful than his eyes. He smiled sadly at her. "I knew you would find me."

Deming walked up to him. Her wings beat against her back. She could choose to appear to him in any form, and came to him as the Angel of Mercy. "Why did you kill them?"

"It's a long story," he said, putting her hand against his cheek.

"Does it begin in Florence? In the fifteenth century?"

Paul's face lit up. "Why yes. You were getting there, weren't you?"

"You saw the Repository files in my bag. You knew I would find out. That's why you conjured the illusion that afternoon. The girl in your car who was meant to be Victoria."

"Mmm-hmm."

"So tell me, what happened in Florence?"

"It's simple, really. Stuart and Victoria were part of a sect. They were called the Petruvians. Ghastly group, really. Butchers. Murderers. The worst kind of slayer. They killed in the name of peace, in the name of justice, in the name of God. They killed my mother."

"They must have had good reason," Deming protested. "The Code of the Vampires would never allow—"

"The Code of the Vampires does not protect the innocent!" Paul snapped. "The Code only serves to protect the vampires. No one else matters."

"You're wrong. The Code was created to protect humans. It always has."

Then Deming realized: the symbol of union in the video. Silver Bloods had mated with human women. Paul Rayburn was demon born, Nephilim. The bastard child of Croatan and Red Blood. "You should not exist," she said. "The vampires were not given the gift of creating life." Even Allegra's daughter was considered Abomination by some of the community. No one knew how Schuyler came into being.

"And yet I do. And I am not the only one. Take heed,

vampire. For you are not the only orphans of the Almighty on this earth."

Paul raised his hand, and Deming could see he was carrying a *zhanmadao*, a two-handed saber that glittered with hellfire. "I am so very sorry, for I did not lie to you about my love, my sweet Venator. But I cannot allow you to live. The Mistress will keep her secrets."

Deming removed the chopsticks from her hair and raised the long sharp blade of Mercy-Killer. "I am sorry as well. My love for you was real."

The demon boy smiled. "Yes, you have made me your familiar. Alas, the *Caerimonia* will not allow you to harm me. My blood is your own."

He was right, of course. The Sacred Kiss ingrained a loyalty in its vampires so that a Blue Blood would never be able to deliberately harm one's familiar after first bite. The biggest danger was in taking a human to Full Consumption because of bloodlust. After the Sacred Kiss was sealed, the human would forever be safe from their vampire.

Deming stared at Paul. His shirt collar was open, and she saw it again. Right at his neck. The triglyph with the symbols from the original hostage video. The sword piercing a star: Lucifer's mark. The sign of union. Last, the image of the lamb.

She had seen it first when she had taken him into her arms and pierced him with her fangs. She had chosen him; she had made him hers. She had done it out of love and duty. He had asked her not to—but only so that her resolution to do exactly what he wanted would be even stronger.

"There's only one problem with that rule," Deming said as she raised her sword. "You're not human." So that was why his blood had tasted strange. The bitterness of it came from the taste of coal and the underworld.

Paul tried to block her with his blade, but her sword cleaved his in two. He gasped and fell to his knees, and for the first time, he looked afraid. "Think of your love for me," he begged.

Deming looked down at him pitilessly. "I am," she told him, and with all the strength she had, she struck her blade deep into his heart.

The Mistress

The highest tower in Florence was the unfinished dome, and once again, Tomi and Gio scaled the masonry to the top of the building.

"There's nothing here," Gio said, shaking his head.

Tomi took one more walk around the edge. She looked up at the night sky through the open ceiling. Then she knelt down and tapped on stone floor. It was hollow. The top of the dome might not be finished, but the floor below it was complete.

"Down the stairs," Tomi said. "Follow me."

The topmost landing was an empty hallway, save for one secret door. Tomi pushed against it, and it opened at her bidding.

Inside, there was a human female. One of the greatest beauties in Florence, whose portrait was painted by many of the city's greatest artists, all of whom were in love with her.

"Simonetta!" Tomi cried. Simonetta de Vespucci was married to a nobleman in the Medici circle and was rumored to be no other than the great Lorenzo de Medici's beloved mistress. She had not been seen

in the city for a while, and now Tomi knew why.

"Do not come near me!" Simonetta cried, protecting her burgeoning belly. She was nine months pregnant.

When she hugged her stomach, Tomi noticed a mark on her arm. It was the same as the one carried by the man from the Citadel.

Simonetta was no mistress to the Medici.

"Who is your lover?" Gio demanded. "Who is the father of your baby?"

Tomi understood what he was really asking—under whose guise does the Dark Prince walk the earth once again? The Morningstar had returned, it was clear. But in whose form?

When Simonetta answered, Tomi was not surprised.

The girl named Andreas as the father of her baby.

PART THE FOURTH

FORKS IN THE ROAD

FORTY-ONE

The Petruvian Order (Schuyler)

*S*chuyler found a small room for MariElena in the northwest corner of Santa Maria del Fiore, in a small hidden ancillary building that housed the Petruvian Order in the Basilica complex. They had arrived in Florence a few hours ago. When Schuyler released him from her compulsion, Ghedi had insisted they take the girl to the priests.

It was a relief to be back in the world again, and the sight of the busy Italian streets, with tourists crammed into the plaza, had invigorated her.

As far as she and Jack could tell, there were very few Petruvians left. They had counted only a handful of priests upon their arrival. The clerics had housed them in a room next to MariElena's, where they waited until the holy men were ready to meet them.

There was a knock on their door, and another young

African priest entered the room. "We are ready for you. Please come with me."

He led them through dark passageways into a simple room. In contrast to the magnitude of the complex, it was a plain room with a table and chairs. Ghedi and two older priests were waiting.

Schuyler and Jack took seats across from them.

"I am Father Arnoldi. I understand that you stopped Father Awale from performing the cleansing rite."

"Cleansing! He was going to kill her," Schuyler protested. "Explain to me how murder is possibly any part of your work."

"When the order was founded by Father Linardi, we were given two directives by the Blessed Ones, and one was the continued purge of the Mistress's children."

"The Mistress?" Jack asked.

The priest nodded. "Lucifer's first human bride. It is said he gave her the gift of eternal life but she was destroyed by the first Petruvians."

"Who are the Blessed Ones?" Schuyler asked.

"The vampires, like yourselves. Our founders."

"You're telling me that Blue Bloods sanctioned the killing of humans? Of innocent women?" Schuyler demanded.

"They have been marked with the triglyph," the priest said, bowing his head. "They carry the Nephilim. For hundreds of years we have held fast to our mission. We guard the gate. We hunt down the contaminated."

"The gate is a lie. Hellsmouth is nothing but a smoke screen. There is no gate there," Schuyler declared.

The priests balked. "It is a sacred space. . . . That cannot be."

"It is," Schuyler said. "We were there."

"You entered the gate." Father Arnoldi looked sharply at Ghedi. "That is not allowed." As Jack had guessed, the human gatekeepers had been ordered to stay away from the site.

Ghedi bowed his head. "It was necessary. The girl was there."

"We were led there. Whoever took MariElena, they wanted us to know it was false," Jack explained. "They are taunting us."

"Ghedi said Father Baldessarre was worried about certain things?" Schuyler asked.

The priests shifted in their seats and looked uncomfortable. "Lately, there have been too many taken. Each year only one, or two at the most. But now we hear too many reports, and each is the same. The girls are taken, and when we find them, they carry the mark."

"You will not kill MariElena," Schuyler warned.

The old priest looked at her balefully. "She carries a dangerous enemy. It is better for her to die."

Schuyler realized something. When they had first asked Ghedi to explain his connection to his grandfather, Ghedi had told them a story of his mother's death. "Ghedi, your mother, she had been taken. . . ."

"Yes." Ghedi nodded. "She carried the mark. It burned in her skin. And her belly grew. She began to have visions and shakes. She spoke of Hell."

"You told us she died in childbirth, and that the priests took you as an orphan. But the Petruvians killed her, didn't they? And took you in afterward."

He did not deny it.

"And yet you do not hate them," she marveled.

"My mother was damned, Schuyler. And the child could not live. Not in this world."

"We will not allow you to harm MariElena," Schuyler said. "There has to be a way to heal her."

The conversation came to a stalemate, and the meeting adjourned. Back in their room, Schuyler rummaged through Lawrence's notes. "I think I found something that links Father Linardi, the first Petruvian, to Catherine of Siena." She held up a sheaf of letters. "I didn't think they were important, but now I do. Jack, these are love letters. Benedictus was Catherine's human familiar. She ordered him to guard this false gate. Which means that the real gate is still somewhere here."

Schuyler tied the sheets excitedly. "Catherine was guarding the real gate, and used the Petruvians as a decoy."

"But the Croatan know the gate is false, and if they are taking women, it means that the real gate, wherever it is, has been compromised somehow," Jack said.

"But if that's the case, wouldn't this whole countryside be overrun with demons already?"

"Not exactly. What did Ghedi say? The raiders who took his mother—the flesh traders who took MariElena—they were human. Michael's strength still keeps the demons in the underworld."

"But it doesn't keep humans out." Schuyler nodded. "They're taking the girls to Hell. That was why I couldn't locate MariElena in the glom."

"We have to find Catherine. We have to tell her what's been happening here. This whole thing must be a mistake. The Blue Bloods can't have allowed this. . . . Michael and Gabrielle would never . . . Something has gone very wrong here.

"We'll find Catherine," Schuyler said resolutely. "I have a feeling she can't be far. Lawrence thought she might be in Alexandria. He had meant to go there, but he'd wanted to check out Father Baldessarre first." She put away her grandfather's papers, and when she looked up, Jack's eyes were bright.

What is wrong, my darling? she sent, and walked over to take his hand. *We are safe. We will fight this horror.*

"I cannot go with you to Egypt," Jack said, gripping her hand tightly.

"What do you mean?"

"There will be more bounty hunters. We got lucky this

time. But I cannot put you in any more danger. I must go back and face Mimi."

Schuyler did not say a word, and held Jack's hand even tighter.

"This is the only way, my love," Jack said. "For the two of us to be free, I must face the blood trial. I could never face myself if you ever came to harm because of me."

Schuyler trembled. "They will burn you," she whispered.

"Do you have so little faith in me?"

"I will go with you," she said, even though she knew she would not. She had to finish her grandfather's work. She had to carry on the legacy. Innocent women and children were being slain in the name of the Blessed.

"No. You know you must not," Jack said.

You said we would never be separated, ever again.

And we will not. Not ever. There is a way to be together always. Jack dropped to his knees and looked up at Schuyler with so much love. "Will you?"

Schuyler gasped and pulled him to his feet. She was ecstatic and devastated at the same time. "Yes. Yes. Of course. Yes."

It was decided, then. Shuyler would look for Catherine of Siena and the true Gate of Promise, while Jack would return to New York to fight for his freedom. But before they went their separate ways, they would seal their bond.

FORTY-TWO

The Road to Hell (Mimi)

Mimi Force looked up at the Repository scribe sitting in front of her. "The Venators have crushed the coup. There will be no disbandment. For now the Coven stands."

"I heard. Congratulations."

"They're going to stick together and stick with me for now." Mimi pursed her lips. "If they know what's best for them."

"I can't imagine you had me fetched from the basement just to crow over your victory, as deserved as it may be."

"You're right; there's something else. The Repository report came in on the blood spell that hit me."

"And?"

"It was not sent by a member of the Conclave, nor from any vampire in this Coven."

"No?"

"No—and it wasn't from the Nephilim that Deming killed either."

"Then who?"

"I don't know. That's what we need to find out. And there was something else," she said. "When the report came in, I also got back the coat I was wearing that day. I found this in it." She showed him a cross, monogrammed with the initials O.H.P. "It's yours, isn't it?"

Oliver nodded.

"You put a talisman in my pocket. The only thing that can deflect a blood spell. I survived because of you."

"I had a feeling you'd need it. But I didn't want to tell you because you probably wouldn't have accepted a talisman from me."

"You're right, I wouldn't have." She would never have believed that protection from a Red Blood could amount to anything. The blood spell was the essence of malice, and a protection was its opposite. It was a form of self-sacrifice—fashioning a talisman meant that whoever gave it went unprotected himself, vulnerable to whatever evil lurked in the universe.

"You don't have to thank me," Oliver said.

"I haven't."

"I mean, it's just my job. Can't have the Regent die on my watch, can I?"

"I suppose not." Mimi couldn't look him in the eyes. He wasn't her type, even though he wasn't bad-looking, and most girls would probably find him cute, with those long bangs and puppy dog eyes. But no—that was not the emotion she was feeling.

She was feeling something else. Gratitude. Affection. She had never felt this way for a boy before. She had experienced desire and lust and the agony of love, but had never fallen in like.

She *liked* him. Oliver, she was beginning to realize, in the space of just a few weeks, was her friend, and she was his. They had never cared for each other in the past, but somehow, because they were both alone and in mourning, he understood where she was coming from, and didn't judge her for her fits of grief and rage. He'd been there. He was feeling it too.

Plus, they worked together well. Because there was no attraction, no tension, they could laugh and tease and joke around. In the middle of this crazy mess, she'd made a friend.

"Don't," he warned.

"Don't what?"

"Don't get all mushy. I still don't like you very much." He smiled.

"I still don't like you very much either," Mimi said, even though she knew they were both lying. Her face softened. "Hey. Thank you. I mean it. Thanks for looking out," she said, trying not to cringe. It was hard for her to owe anyone anything, most of all a human.

"I did a little digging around the Repository files. I thought you might find this interesting. According to the Book of Spells, a *subvertio* does not kill the immortal spirit. It only consigns them to the deepest circle of the Underworld."

Mimi put the gold cross away. "Tell me something I don't know."

"Listen, if you can find a gate and walk down the Path of the Dead, you can get him out. He can't do it on his own. But with the Angel of Death, he may be able to," Oliver said excitedly.

"There's just one thing: who knows where the other gates are? I don't have time to go on another wild goose chase."

"I went through the rest of Lawrence Van Alen's notes again. I think there's a real possibility that the Gate of Promise isn't in Florence, but in Alexandria."

"Why are you telling me this?" Mimi asked.

"The Venators have found your brother. He's left Florence. Jack refuses to turn himself in to them. He says he'll only submit to you. And he's alone."

"I saw that report," Mimi said. "You are very crafty, my friend. My brother returns to the city to face his fate, and so you dangle hope that I might find Kingsley, in order to get me out of town. Why do you even care? With Jack out of the way, she won't have a choice but to return to you."

"We can be in Cairo by nightfall," Oliver said, ignoring Mimi's taunting.

"We?" She raised an eyebrow.

"You'll need backup."

"So . . . all roads lead to Hell." She rested her head on her hands. She could go to Egypt and rescue her love, or she could stay in New York and face her brother and sentence him to death.

"Well? I doubt Kingsley is enjoying himself down there."

Mimi stood up. "Pack your bags. We'll leave tonight. Tell the Venators to hold my brother until I return. I'll deal with him then. Who says I can't kill two birds with one stone?"

Mimi smiled. She would have her love. Then she would have her revenge.

Forty-three

Hunter and Hunted (Deming)

*P*aul Rayburn was dead. He had exacted his vengeance on his mother's killers, but Deming had brought him to justice. She had done what she had set out to do. She felt the pain of his death in her blood and in her soul, but her determination was resolute. She faced the twin Venators sitting opposite from her. "He said there are others like him in the world. We must find them."

Sam Lennox nodded. "Where will you begin your hunt?"

"I went through his file. His passport was filled with stamps from the Middle East. That's where I'll start," she said. The Nephilim did not cycle through reincarnations. Their demon provenance made them Enmortal.

"Are you with me?" she asked the brothers.

"It beats staying around here waiting for Jack Force to show up." Ted shrugged. "I'll talk to the Regent, have another team assigned to that case."

"Good. My sister will join us once we arrive." She smiled. "You'll like her. She's just like me."

"Oh great," Sam said, exchanging a meaningful look with his brother. "There's two of them."

Acknowledgments

Thank you to the family, especially my husband and collaborator, Mike Johnston, and our baby girl, Mattie (who isn't a baby anymore but will always be our baby). Thank you to the DLC and Johnston families and all our extendeds. We love you.

Thank you to my dear friends who supported me during the worst year of my life. Thank you to my publishing family at Hyperion, especially my editors and champions, Jennifer Besser, Christian Trimmer, and Stephanie Lurie; and my publicist and marketing gurus, Jennifer Corcoran and Nellie Kurtzman, who have been taking care of me from the beginning of my YA career. Thank you to my agent and best advocate, Richard Abate.

I also want to extend a very special thank you to Dr. Luis Martinez, Dr. Steven Applebaum, Dr. Ramin Khalili, Dr. Cary Manoogian, and to all their nurses and office staff who took care of my dad during his battle with cancer, especially Stacey Christ, Kim Medeiros, Michelle Huber, Emma Martinez, Diane Saenz, Jessica Osorio, Vivian Montes, and Rose Ramirez. Thank you all for everything you did for Pop—our family will always treasure the loving care you provided, and we thank you from the bottom of our hearts for the six "bonus years" he enjoyed.